Tilsa Wri~

Lady in Red

Federal Agents keep watching!

from the author. The only exception is by a reviewer, who may quote short excerpts in a review.

Printed in the United States of America
First Printing:

Cover design credit: Randel Pearson, Brooklyn based freelance artistic talented designer. Follow him on Instagram @randydezign4u, join
his Facebook fan page: Pearson Designs

Why this story? One word, true answer, Notorious BIG! Oh yeah, back in August 2012, I decided to listen to my CD collection. After rocking to Biggie's Life After Death, a scene popped and my laptop was right in front of me waiting. Within four hours or so, I had written four or five chapters free flow, no outline just pure writing from the top of my head.

With that said, I will declare that this entire story is fictional and most importantly if you already have this album, it wouldn't hurt to purchase another copy. I like Biggie for being so brave, so creative and most importantly setting the standard without even trying hard. His contribution will never be broken or over looked. I salute him for being himself.

They say art is life and Biggie's life was truly artistic!

#Brooklyn

Author Tilsa C. Wright

Taking this opportunity to acknowledge and express my gratitude for the only four men who mean THE WORLD to me! Hance Jackson, Rohan Davis, Shawn Brooks and finally my very special favorite Kirkland Davis. Thank you for standing with me regardless of my flaws.

Chapter 1
Pacifier Drips Milk

"Lady in red why are you not talking to me?" I turned around looking at him dead in his eyes to his usual game; they called him King Phil. He sure was giving me some street lyrics, each time I walked on East 95th and Rutland Road, King Phil had something smart to say. I swear he was clocking me each time. I liked the attention but he was a serious gangster, a gangster who addressed me with a proper dialogue. No 'hey ma', nor 'hey b', like some other young cats would.

"Give me a reason to talk to you King!"

"So now I am your King; after how many weeks of you ignoring me?"

"Well since you address me like a Queen, I acknowledge your status as King, not my King but the King of the streets."

"That sentence had too many Kings; just call me Phil, for I plan to fill you up someday." I couldn't resist his charm. I burst out laughing, I was lost for words. He got me good. As I walked away from Phil, my thoughts shift to my boyfriend of five years, Pablo Rodney. He was waiting for me upstairs. I love the idea of Pablo being jealous. However, a fresh cup of Phil would be good. I have had the same strokes since 16 and I know there is more to life than what Pablo offered.
"Took you long enough Keisha!" My mother yelled as she stood in the apartment front door way.

"Hush mother, next time you climb these steps and get your special red peas to cook, rice and peas." This woman can get on my nerve; she's short, heavy weight from all the West Indian dishes she cooks every day. Yes every day, she feeds her son-in-law Pablo. Well she regards him as such. I have grown tired of him. Always some chick calling my phone, or investigating about our relationship; the last straw for me is Destiny Chambers. Destiny recently had his son, four month old Pablo Rodney Jr.

As I entered the apartment I smelled the curry goat bubbling in the pot. "Mom cook some shrimp for me nuh, and the goat for Pablo, please?" I asked as there was some frozen shrimp in the freezer.

"Go from here, I cooking for me and my son. The Chinese restaurant, Dragon House has your fried shrimp vegetable rice waiting."

"Keisha, come here!" Pablo shouted. Sorry ass Mr. Pablo demanded my presence in the living room, where he was sitting counting stacks of cash.

"What can I do for you, Pablo?" I asked disinterested as I stood in the living room blocking the 40 inches Sony television.

"We are going to VA tonight. I have a drop to make and I need you to ride with me."

"No, find someone else. I am done with this game." This was the fourth time he asked and I refused; either he was slow or just plain out right stupid.
"Oh really now, so how will the bills get paid around here, who will clothe and feed you? No hustle no money, no

money no nothing." Pablo was sure to point out his contributions and how important he is to our household.

I remained silent; his temper flares up for the simplest things. Hissing my teeth I walked towards my bedroom and once inside I quickly locked the door. Five minutes later, I hear Pablo on his cell, not sure who he was talking to or about what.

"Yeah let her come tonight, we have room; does she look the part?" I got up off the chair and stood with my ear glued to the door, trying to hear clearer, who would be the girl in Red to ride with him tonight. I thought to myself, hope she knows the game well enough to not get caught and send the ring to prison for years without end.

"I know that Shorty, she's from Sound View Projects. She is good money, see you guys around 10." He said to the person on the other line.

Like a broken record he went over minor details about the drop before hanging up and heading for my room. He was knocking or more like banging it down for me to open the door. Sound View Projects, that's where I met Pablo five years ago, when I was 16. He has been dealing since then. Now our relationship is stale like the cheese on the mice trap set in the kitchen behind the fridge. This scene of me and him arguing is so played out. He fails to realize that I no longer want him; going through the motions of sleeping with him, is just to appease my mother. My pimp mother, who knows of his daily living, doesn't care as long as she gets her house money and other perks. He was a provider, a means to an end, just that it was my end getting slapped and poked each night from this beast; he enjoyed riding me rough.

In the hood most mothers are just like her, a real female mother hen pimp. "Pablo leave please I am begging you, please, I am not in the mood to argue with you."
"I don't want to argue either Keke, just want to talk with my baby before I leave out for VA." I opened the door; like a fool, he walked in slams the door and then locks it.

"What is really going on here Keisha?"

"I don't want you anymore Pablo, I'm done!" Boy was I foolish to have said that, Pablo slapped me in the face; my right ear rang louder than the Catholic Church bell on a Sunday.

"So you had an abortion Keisha?" He raised his voice; you could stay four blocks from my apartment building and hear the commotion. One would expect my dear mother to come to my rescue, too much expectation for she always tunes out our arguments. She plays conveniently deaf if you ask me.

"Yes, I aborted your two timing, drug dealing seed!" Across my ears, this slap connected my left. I screamed and yelled in agony, guess my mother's ear drum unclogged. She beat down the door, Pablo was now pinning me down on the bed, ripping my clothes off.

"Pablo, stop! I am bleeding Pablo." I had the procedure two days ago and I was bleeding miserably. Like the monster he is, he didn't stop. He unzipped his pants, pulled me by my hair and forced my mouth open to suck him. "She is ok Moms, she's just fine; nothing a big girl pacifier cannot fix." He assured my mother.

8

"Ok, you kids need to behave, there is no need for all the noise." That's all mother hen said, like an uncaring, hands off school teacher afraid to lose her licenses.

He leans in over and whispers in my ringing right ear, "Your baby is fine Ms. Carmen; she is sucking a pacifier with a little milk for vitamin and nourishment." Where did this animal come from? Pablo never spoke like this. Our sex life never comprised of me giving him oral, only if I wanted to, he never forced his two timing tools of trade down my throat. Oh God why me?

I had to orally please him, as if I wanted to taste his juice or as he just told mother his pacified milk. Tears running down my cheeks, one day this will end I told myself and that day was now! I swear if he tries to comeback in my life after this, I am going to move so far away from New York, not even the Feds will be able to find me. I am done with him!

"Now abort that, abort my sperms from down your throat bitch!" Pablo was cruel, bitter and disgusting. I cowardly cried but no sound came from my wind pipes. I had to swallow his ejaculation. He got up from the bed, changed his clothes went into the living room and returned to my bedroom.

"Here, take this!" He insisted I take the hand full of cash. I looked away. I couldn't force my hand to take it. I felt cheap, rotten, like a filthy washcloth.

"This is the last you will see of me and my drug dealing money!" He said as he walked out the bedroom and headed for the front door.

Good riddance it took both ears ringing like Big Ben in London, an abortion and nasty oral sex to get him out my life. This cycle of abuse in my family needs to end, long gone the times I thought when a man showers you with money and gifts, it means he loves, respects and values you. My mother didn't know any better; my father Roberto Lopez was from Puerto Rico lived in South Bronx where he met my mother then Carmen Williams who was born in Portland Jamaica West Indies.

Carmen couldn't read or write. She had a hard life. The only thing she knew is men taking care of women and having children. Her philosophy was, the more children you had for a man, the likelihood of him staying and taking care of you. This was so back in the 40's or 50's; nowadays men hump and jump leaving you on welfare with years of stress. One of my mother's Aunt, we called her Auntie-B for short, her name was Betty Williams. Auntie-B helped my mother to get a visa to travel the United States and to return, well she came and instead of listening to her Aunt, she met my father and began having children and overstayed.

Roberto Lopez died before I was born. He was a handsome ladies man who treated my mother like a door mat. Mother had my older sister Roberta a year after she came to America; it was hard for her to get work and support my sister and herself with no work permit. My father being the player and dope dealer took care of his other women who had something going on for themselves or could give him handouts, but my mother got scrap meat to support her and my sister.

Being the naive woman she was then and she is still today, my mother got pregnant for my father again, this time boring twin boys, Carlos and Carlito who are both dead as a result of following my father's footsteps. My other set of twin brothers, Raymond, and Rodriquez are presently serving time at a Missouri State Correctional Prison. They were caught transporting a trunk full of coke along with $100,000 cash. After their 15 years sentence, they will be deported back to Jamaica. Both were unfortunate to have born there. How come? Well after having the first sets of twins, mother got into some immigration problems and had to return to Jamaica. She left the twins and Roberta with her Auntie-B, hoping that her situation would change in less than a year, since my father reluctantly married her only two months before her immigration Attorney got her case in the hopes of her winning a quote on quote Green Card Lottery.

He should have married her before Roberta was born and at least filed for her then. The long and short of this story is that my father visited her in Jamaica after being there for three years. He was being a knuckle head running the streets and totally ignoring my mother's plea for help. Auntie-B decided to pressure my father and threaten child support, so he mustered up the courage and went to Jamaica to my mother's aide. Needless to say she got pregnant and had Raymond and Rodriquez in Jamaica before getting the proper documents to return to America.

So as to not confuse you, as I was at some stage of my life, my sister Roberta is now 35, my deceased twin brothers would have been 33 and the incarcerated twins are 28 same age as Pablo and I am the baby, or wash belly as mother likes to call me at times is 21, a born New Yorker.

Chapter 2
Double Pound Cakes

Monday morning, too tired to get out of bed or even talk on the phone with my one and only girlfriend Jessica Valez. Jay as we affectionately called her lives 2 blocks from me. I live on 95th and Rutland, she lives on 92nd. She was the only girl I talked to around here, most of the other females are Jamaicans, always wilding out on the streets, cursing over men and who dresses better than the other. Jay called me several times. I pressed the ignore button, just needed my own head space for couple hours. Mother has been nagging me about money. She knows me very well, that pimp knows I have a couple thousand stashed in the house. After all I am no fool, my big brother Raymond taught me to save money while dealing with Pablo.

He said to me before he got locked up, "Sis if Pablo gives you $1000 to go shopping, spend $600 and save $400. He might find another woman and leave you dry someday, never let him know you have stash, always tell him you are on E-empty."

Pablo was good with money. He gave me $2000 each month for my pockets, and mother $800 for the house and out of respect for my brother Raymond. Pablo and Raymond were very close; back then my brother had the bright idea to transport dope out West, while Pablo wanted to play it safe and keep his business local. Not sure what happened why now Virginia seems to be his running State. I had $20,000, 15 in the house and 5 in the bank, at 21 without a proper job there was no way I can tell the Feds I earned and saved 20 cakes. Besides 10 cakes was an automatic red flag by law, told you I was street smart. I had to learn and learn real fast. My brothers had stash all over Sound View, after they got clipped in Missouri, mother and I were financially okay for about two years. They made sure we were cared for. Plus Pablo and I were head over heels in love with each other then, his allowance was small at first, but as soon as he came into more dope money, my allowances increased and my skin caught fire for his rough sex. Yes the rough sex that was the only way Pablo knew how to do his screwing in the bedroom.

Pablo paid more attention to me during the first three years of our relationship. He took me places out of town, casinos and nice hotels just to chill and see life differently from the hood. Things changed as soon as he started making it big and Destiny his now baby moms decided to try me, since I lived in another borough, Brooklyn and she lived in Bronx. Destiny and her friends had tons of mouth strength since there was distance between our dwelling places.

Actually she lives in my old neighborhood. Pablo was mostly hanging out there during the day since that's where his business was based. He pinched her buns during the day time and bangs me each night. All this was news to me. During her pregnancy, this jump off harassed my phone looking for him after she got knocked up. Destiny and her gang of chicken head girlfriends left Bronx, drove to my block to curse me and Pablo out. Can you believe the nerve of some younglings, now she can have him; we are officially done.

Mother and I moved to Brooklyn after my brothers' stash money ran out. We decided to keep a low profile from where we were hot and in the sights of the new drug ring. Furthermore we had no guaranteed protection anymore.

13

Of course Pablo would protect us but why bother put him through the hassle when he was taking care of us and building his crew trying to move heavy weight out of State.

We left from one hood to the next, same drug infested streets; only difference is in the Bronx we were around mostly Spanish and here in Brooklyn Jamaicans ruled the 90's. King Phil was one of the bosses around this cut, who just happened to have his sexual eyes on me the second I moved here.

"Get out of bed you lazy bomb!" My short fused mother came charging in the room, yelling like a crazy woman from a mental hospital.

"Ma, what's wrong with you, can I get some sleep woman!"

"No! Get up, I need money to pay the rent and since you ran Pablo my kitty jar is low. So you either hand over some money now or I am renting your room to strangers."

"We at this same topic about money again Ma, every day you nag me for money like a pimp! Why not dress me in red and put me on the track over there in East New York?" She said nothing and disappeared somewhere. This woman was off her medication or something. The next thing I know she came in the room with a broom stick and gave me a slap across my back. I damn near saw the stars at 9 o'clock in the morning.

"Was that bloody necessary? I am tired of your money hungry, pimping ass I am taking my clothes, had enough of your bull crap. I'm out!"

I know better than to fight back. She was my mother and no matter the circumstances I loved her, I totally get her

14

not knowing any better. So instead of fighting and disrespecting her further I decided it was time to leave her crib. Let her fend for herself, it's time she got a wakeup call and stand on her own.

"Jay, sorry about earlier, was just holding a strong and deep meditation. Mama Dukes jack me up again, went in on me with a broom stick!"

"What? Are you kidding me?"

"No, I need to jam by you for couple days while I sort out my living situation."

"Sure, no worries you can stay for a week, my Moms won't mind at all."

The word situation was a code for where to stash my cash safely; sometimes making a hurried move can cost you all your loot. Having nothing in the hood, is like being dead or homeless on the streets with a cardboard box for a bed and one dollar bottle vodka for dessert after left over Chinese food scrap from pitying strangers.

"Keke, have you heard from Pablo since the incident?" I could tell she didn't want to bring the subject up, not sure why she did anyhow.

"No, not one word of Spanish or English from that punk."
"What time you coming with your stuff?"

"Hmmm not sure around 4, I might have to run a quick errand before heading to your crib."

"Do you need me to come with you?"

"No I got this, nothing serious just a quick situation." She must get the picture by now. I trust her but not to the extent of telling her every God damn thing. Besides I need to stash these 15 cakes, not sure what on earth to do, yes this street smart kid was out of answers. Damn you mother for messing up my money game!

It was summer time, streets literally hot, with all sorts of drama and the temperature made it even more worst. 1 pm, King Phil is usually on the corner checking the undercover checking him out. Not sure why he did this but I guess it made sense to him, for they never caught him doing any transaction, or searched him and found contraband. They always come up empty handed and would say to him one day they will get lucky.

"Lady in red I see you walking towards me." Phil and his junk lyrics or small talk, whichever I wasn't feeling it. I made serious eye contact, sending a message letting him know I needed to talk business not fool around.

I need to move these cakes by any means necessary. There was no way I would take this cash by Jay's house. Her boyfriend's nickname was 10 fingers Tommy; believe me he can rob you with his hands folded behind in cuffs. That dude was as good as it gets, when jacking people up in the streets.

Using minimal body language, I stepped inside the Ire Jamming Jamaican restaurant on the corner, ordered an oxtail lunch special and sat; eating slowly hoping Phil would get the drift to come inside and small talk. I don't want to be seen by the undercover talking to him in the streets. That's too much evidence or reason to come knocking on my door later on. The restaurant had regulars, no strangers, or snitches. He came in, ordered a small chicken foot soup. To my surprise, a young lady wearing a red top similar to mine tapped me on the shoulder.

"Walk to the back, I will sit here until you return." She whispered softly. We did it so quickly; the UC (Under Cover) wouldn't have noticed our body double just like in the movies, besides the restaurant had tinted windows for keeping out the sun and other peeping eyes. Phil really had his game tight; I would say 99% air tight.

"Lady in red, what do you want?" He got to the point.

"I got 10 cakes and need a reproducing bakery to cut and double."

"Funny, here I thought you were an innocent pretty Spanish girl, who didn't want me having her." He said licking his lips suggestively, I could tell he was undressing me with his weed shot eyeballs.

"It's never too late for a shower of rain on the right head, for a long term package deal with no competition." I decided to give him riddles, needed to see how smart he really was. Jamaicans speak different street slang than us Bronx Spanish cats in the hood.

"Funny, I was thinking the same, since you are now solo, no Spanish Papa or Virginia Slims." He looked me dead in the eyes, very cold and serious. Phil knew my personal business.

"Is 10 all you have?" I could tell he was testing me, wanting to see my hand before the shuffle.
"Yes, I am stepping two blocks left for 7 stars, after which and new view for good."

"How soon do you need to reproduce, chicken takes time to hatch."

"Who said anything about chickens? I am into baking using white flour; the other colors are not acceptable for me. I need to know if you can double cakes in 5 stars and then take 5 cakes off the machinery for the head baker."

"I knew there was a reason I liked you."

We both laughed, exchanged cell numbers and kept it moving. I did the body switch and played around my plate. Not sure if this chick left any unwanted guests in my food while I was in the back conducting business.

I got up disposed of my food and calmly walked back to mother's. Started packing my necessities, I had no choice but to travel light. Jay didn't have plenty space to hold all my clothes and shoes much less my other belongings. One hour later, Phil text me a code, within seconds there was a knock on my front door. Damn I never buzzed the building front door, who the hell is that I wondered to myself.

"Who is it?" I asked gingerly, scared out my panties; after all I just told the man of the streets who I really don't know that I had 10 cakes in my apartment.

"Girl let me in; I got flour on my shoes from the bakery." And that was the code. I let him in, a short handsome looking cat, he looked so simple not hood with beads or nothing remotely gangster on his body. Not even a tattoo, nor smelled of neither weed nor crack, a clean soldier. He was a serious cat. I flirted with him to ease the tension but he ignored me. I took him to my room, mother left for the store, so it was just me and him alone in the apartment.

Handing over my cash was nerve wracking but I had no other choice. Just like that a street soldier walked out my apartment with 10 cakes.

"Keke, what time are you coming over?" Jay was on the other end of my cell phone.

"In 30 to 45 minutes, why you so pressed for time? My radar or better yet my street instinct was very sharp when it comes on to my money. I had 5 cakes on me, her man was 10 fingers Tommy, although she is cool, I had to be four steps ahead of her and not to mention him and his boys. So I decided to stop in Chase on Utica Avenue deposit 2 cakes, leave my pimp mother hen 1 cake, and roll with 2 until I got a spot for myself, or at least figure out my next move.

Just as I thought, as I drove in a taxi towards Jay's house there she was with her man and two other cats on the steps. Looking hungry and up to no good. I told the driver, whose car windows were tinted to continue driving, the Bronx was my last resort. From the look of things on Jay's steps, she could have been trying to set me up and not having my brothers or Pablo to defend me in the streets, the less heat I brought to myself the better at this point.

"Baby girl, little Keke, I need for you to lay low, stop rolling with Pablo. I know he is doing right by you financially, but that Lady Red game is not what I want for you sis." Raymond's exact words to me 7 months ago, when mother and I went to visit my brothers in Missouri State Correctional Prison.
Although my brothers were on the West Coast or close enough out west, they heard all the latest street news, who is pounding who and who is calling the shots in the Bronx. Pablo had moved up in ranks, and so did another crew; they ran the streets going by the name, *Leggos*. Not sure

what it meant, nor did I care, I just know when my brother Raymond gave me an order I listened.

On my way to the Bronx, Jay called me at least 50 times; this chick was blowing up my phone. Damn she made it so obvious. Goes to show you cannot trust anyone, not even slightly, come to think of it, how did King Phil know about me and Pablo breaking up? We talked in code at the restaurant, which was the very first time I had a one on one with him. So funny now that I think more about it. I told her about Pablo leaving me but never about our *Lady Red* code. *Lady Red* was Pablo's bright idea, which he got from me loving to wear red. It's a long story but let me just give you a quick rundown.

My father died before I was born and at that time my mother was living in the Bronx, she met some spiritual people who called themselves Yoruba Orishas Warriors. I am not sure why, but she took me to one of the Babalawo who instructed her that Shango was my protector and also red is my color. Ever since then I always wore something red and each year like clockwork, until I was 16 my mother took me to see the Babalawo who did spiritual rituals to ensure Shango's protection for the remainder of my life. I went along with whatever made my mother happy. I was her wash belly and she considered me the last token from her union with my father.

This is where Pablo got the bright idea to use red when doing his drug transactions. The few times I ran with him to Virginia I wore either a red shoe, or a blouse; hence the label *Lady Red*.

Chapter 3
Mad Money in the Bronx

Roberta Lopez, my big sister lives in the Bronx and although my plan has changed from staying at Jay's, I prefer to stay in a shelter than to spend a night by her. She has 5 kids, with four different men; she is so project living happy I just cannot understand why she would put herself through so many men who refuse to support her and the kids. Why? Uncle Sam has a rent subsidized apartment for her lazy ass, provides her with food stamps and free health insurance for her and these 5 kids. I am very supportive of my family, don't ever get it twisted. Raymond taught me about heavy weight situations that keep you from progressing to the next level and depending on Government assistance can be more of a weight than actual help. Following in mother's footprints was not the way for me, perhaps Roberta, just not me. Again I am not knocking it, I just sometimes feel these programs were designed to keep minorities at one level doing the same thing; like a hamster running on a wheel without an end.

So where in the bloody Bronx will I spend at least one night to gather my thoughts and clear my head. I needed a precise bullet proof plan of action. I'm on my own now, no brothers to back me, no boyfriend to give me a weekly allowance, just me against the odds.

"Driver do you mind taking me to the Bronx, I will make it worth your while! The cab ride to the Bronx is usually $60 plus the toll I was willing to drop $100 given that the original car ride was supposed to be a Brooklyn pick up and drop off. Not all taxi drivers like going out of their borough, some view it as stepping outside their safety zone and being open to robbery at the very least. "How much you talking about young lady? It is a very expensive ride plus I charge extra for gas. This Haitian driver was trying to feed his 20 kids or what!

"Well I have $80." I shot back.

"Not including the toll, give me $90 and I take you to the Bronx with no problem." Game recognize game, I had him right in my ball park.

"We have a deal. I'm going to the Ramada Hotel on Baychester Avenue; do you think you can find it?"

"Of course, I know everywhere in New York." With a very heavy accent he assured me, still wasn't convinced though. One hour and fifteen minutes later we drove up in front of the Ramada; just as I thought this driver had no clue. The Bronx was a maze for him. Thank God I made it safe and sound, just hope I get a decent room, a nice meal, a shot of Hennessy and a good night's rest.

I must have lost track of time it was 11:30 pm not sure when I fell asleep from the stress from my mother and the clear robbery set up Jay and her man had planned for me. I am just glad I was able to divert and out of the line of drama, well at least for a day or two. Not sure how long I can afford the Ramada. King Phil better come through for me in five days or else I have to find a cave to rest my head. Good luck finding a cave these days, shoot. No, what am I saying; this self-pity party is not going to work, no, not at all. Anyways back to sleep I go. God please let me at least dream something big and worry not until morning comes.

"Good morning Keisha Lopez." I said to myself, standing in front of the mirror examining my naked beautiful curvaceous body. Picture my brown complexion, 5'5 tall, a 28 waist line, swollen breasts well from being pregnant for Pablo, glad I terminated that bad seed. Back to my body structure, hips, thick legs and a backside like Jennifer Lopez. We shared more than just a last name we had assets; the only difference is I lacked insurance she didn't.

"With a perfect body, that men seem to always stop while in traffic looking at me in lust, and yet why is my life in such a shamble?" another self-evaluating question. "I need help! But from who or where, another sexual submissive relationship is not the answer, however a temporary solution."

Poor mirror must be wondering why this girl is talking out loud to me, and I cannot give answers. My first night at the Ramada was great. I turned my cell phone off; I didn't want to think about my stressful situations, I just slept. It's the next day and I decided to roam the streets a bit. Auntie-B owned several houses in the Bronx and two Jamaican restaurants and I plan to visit her today for certain.

Auntie-B had three girls. I wasn't close to them, and in fact Auntie-B cut my mother off due to her lack of ambition. Kelly her oldest daughter was around 50 or close enough, lives in Poughkeepsie New York and practices Law. Kelly's daughter Kamejah, Auntie-B's granddaughter, who I did have a chance to meet some years ago for the first time. If I am not mistaken she is about five or six years older than me. Last I heard she owned a Hair Salon off White Plains Road and was doing well for herself.

Auntie-B's other two daughters Wendy and Pamela lives in England, and both worked for the British Government; at least that's what brother Raymond told me. My mother's children were 180 degrees of separation when it comes on to having a stable sound or bloody near productive life when you really compare us. The mirror would never hold up, it would shatter to pieces. I am searching for the balance. I have tons of WHYS? There were times I had resented Auntie-B for shutting us out because of our mother's short comings. But my brother Raymond mentioned that I should go searching for Auntie-B and her children and try my best to be good like them and not end up behind bars or dead. He pleaded with me, to the point it sounded like fingernails on a chalkboard.

A resume', what is that? A sheet of paper containing my work history, oh, ok. How do I write mine? A girl growing up with pains, street tough experiences, had confidence being bold and gangster in the hood; however standing before folks with stature I crumble. I feel less than worthy for their time, my self-esteem buried immediately whenever I walked into a place that had quote on quote progressive people which only happened a few times. It was as though I had a split personality, one minute I am a Superior chick, and yet an inferior dumb chick would surface. A jungle, hard concrete jungle, that's what life is. Finding a middle ground, a conscious mind, a spiritual connection with the universe, Raymond has been writing me letters from Prison, telling me to search for the meaning. Apparently he was attending church services whenever the guards had approved for him to participate. He said he read books. He did whatever trade skills he could get involved in for he was determined to be a better person when he comes out.

"The street game will eat you alive baby girl, being locked up breaks you mentally, only the strong survives in here, only the strong." Raymond's word, my brother was actually getting through to me; it was as though he was here with me on the outside of freedom land. God knows I needed a voice of reasoning and a sense of direction. All my 21 years, I thought I knew life; instead I knew devaluation of worth, my worth was valued with sex, brand name clothes, jewelry, and material sense of security and no assured footing.

'Auntie-Bee's Bar and Grill' I guess this is it, her place of business. I was always in the South Bronx with my Spanish heritage, never around Jamaicans until mother and I moved to Brooklyn, the area her restaurant was located, most people considered it little Jamaica. White Plains Roads and the 200's you will find nothing but Jamaicans and almost everything about the culture.

The smell of curry goat, and other types of food cooking, is one aspect of the culture I was very familiar with. Mother cooked her Jamaican food all the time, so you know other than getting her hips and ass gene, her cooking helped full out my thickness. Looking around at the decorations, this restaurant was very welcoming and not to mention busy with customers. I stood noticeably at the side, not wanting to be served but to speak with whoever was in charge.

"How can I help you?" A not so friendly young lady asked in a very flat non caring voice.

"I am looking for the owner, Miss Betty."

"What's your name and the purpose of you being here?" Again this chick needs a check or to be decked with my fist. She comes across so unprofessional, as though I am here to beg Auntie-B food or money; this chick was even sizing up my clothes and shoes. Home girl better recognize I am not the one; I will mop her backward Jamaican ass to the floor and leave her on the curb for sanitation to scrape up in the morning.

"My name is Keisha Lopez, her niece."
"Oh, okay, give me a second." So now her body language changed as she walked to the back. I tell you most Jamaican restaurant workers' attitude in Brooklyn mirror hers. The few times I purchased food from them is when mother decided she didn't feel like cooking, some of the workers' mannerism is a serious turn off, believe me if the food wasn't tasting good; they would never get my business.

Thinking the worker would reappear from the same door, well I guess not. She snuck up on my right, from the front door and instructed me to follow her. Aunt Betty was three buildings away from the restaurant; actually she was getting her hair done.

"Keisha Lopez, where are you from?" She asked with big bulging eyes looking through her thick Gucci lens.

"South Bronx originally, but recently was living in Brooklyn." I answered, hoping she will be able to connect the dots.

"South Bronx." She repeated. "South Bronx." Again, she was getting up in age so I guess repetition helps the memory cells.

"Oh my niece Carmen daughter Keke, is that really you? Yes, the bulb went on in her head, she got it right on the first try.

"Yes Auntie Betty that would be me."

"Pickney come here! Come hug your Auntie!" Just like that, she made me feel like the prodigal son from the Bible. "Kam! Kam! Come meet your little cousin Keke, Carmen wash belly." Auntie-B was excited, I was afraid her dentures would fall out. Man her jaw was moving around, or was it the dentures, whichever something seemed loose.

"Look at your hair, so beautiful, is that Spanish blood from your father side? Turn 'round let me see you Chile." She had me smiling, feeling like a little girl participating in a beauty pageant on stage spinning, twirling and smiling for the judges. Nothing but love and positivity I felt from this woman, such a huge difference from my own birth mother. Couldn't tell the last time mother hugged me, much less told me I was beautiful.

 Kamejah was inside a room, she came out with a puzzled look on her face; guess the excitement had her stop whatever she was doing.

"Hi, how are you?" Kamejah was much more pleasant than the worker from the restaurant.

"I am fine, nice to see you again Kamejah."

"Yes! I don't remember you."

"Some years ago, my brother Raymond drove by to see you briefly, couple days after you opened the Salon."

"Yes, yes, now I remember you. You look so much different now."

"I was around sixteen when you saw me then."

"Boy how times flies, and we aging yes, sorry to hear about Raymond. How is he doing by the way?" You could tell she had genuine concern about my brother.

"He is strong, as strong as anyone can be in his situation, however in due time he will be in Jamaica living a great life well according to his words. *"Enjoying the beautiful nature of the island, food, music and of course women."* We both laughed at his optimism, which basically covered the void of pain and sadness having a loved one behind bars for so long.

"You young people get acquainted; it's time for The Young and The Restless." Auntie-B was hooked on her soaps, typical retiree syndrome. Soaps, talk shows, game shows, that's their primetime television entertainment, nothing else seems to interest them.

"Keke, come in the back I am doing inventory. Let Granma enjoy her soaps."

Kamejah and I talked a bit. I got right down to business. Told her I needed a place, a job and to find my true purpose in life. There was no need to discuss mother and the drama of my past years, from the looks of things Auntie-B's side of family already knew what we went and is still going through. As brother Raymond insisted I seek help from them to change a pattern or cycle my mother and Roberta seems to love and continue to live in.

Well not to my surprise she owned her house on Baychester Avenue, right by the number 5 train station, the second to last stop to be correct. She made me an offer I couldn't refuse, free lodging for 3 months, while I worked at the Salon as a shampoo girl and she will teach me how to do hair, a small weekly payout and whatever tips I earn will all be mine. Now this was a real game plan, a serious eye opener, new beginning, with great possibilities!

Chapter 4
Bedroom Bully

I left Kam's Beauty Spa, that's the name of her business and headed for the Ramada to gather my belongings. Excited, thankful, talking to the mirror that gave me confidence in the morning, this must be a kind of self-help therapy method. Mirror talking and naked body examination, who would have thought. Anyways it helped me today, I will damn near do it each day if I have to, between my brother Raymond and this mirror talk therapy, as the saying goes, 'something got to give'.

My cell phone alert went off as soon as I came out the shower, there was a voicemail message. I dried my body quickly, since the air conditioner was on, I refused to get sick; got practically half way dressed and then listened to message.

"Hello Keke thought you were coming to stay at my house. At the very least you could have called and told me you changed your mind, some friend you are!" Jay, the pretender, she had a point I should have called but why give thieves a heads up, makes no damn sense if you ask me. I deleted her message, finished getting dressed and checked out of the Ramada; checking out to basically checking into what I considered and hope to be a better life!

Kamejah said I will stay in her basement, which by the way was completely renovated and furnished, just that there was no stove; so if I felt like cooking upstairs in her area, that is where I had to do it. That was the least of my worries, having a peaceful place to sleep, a steady income to look forward to each week, the only thing that should concern me really is King Phil. I almost forgot about my 10 cakes, too overwhelmed with joy.

"Here are your set of keys for the basement Keke, all I am begging you is to not lose them." Kamejah was very serious.

"The stress of changing the locks is too much hassle for me right now."

"I promise to be very careful." I reassured her. My new place! Oh what a feeling, when you dancing on the ceiling, remember that Lionel Richie song? Keisha Maria Lopez was dancing to a new life.

Here comes another WHY? Why mother never listen to Auntie-B when she came to America, well at least the second time around, or even after having me? Mama is a real hard head, my brothers and I, oh even Roberta could have had a better opportunity to make sense of our lives; instead we made absolute nonsense. The buck stops here with me. I intend to change this loser cycle; it will be upward from this moment.

Oh my goodness, Kamejah's house looked like pages from magazines, totally fabulous! Expensive furniture, top of the line kitchen appliances, her bedroom was huge, with a walk in closet. My bedroom was below hers not a good thing from a long term point of view, but who cares. As for my room, same size as the one in Brooklyn, just smaller windows and definitely no mother hen pimping and nagging presence. Kamejah really have it made, business must be very good for her to accumulate so many things, well not just things, but quality things. She has excellent taste and seems to be happy with her life achievements, then again who wouldn't be? When you think about it, Kamejah has it made thanks to her working very hard for it!

"So do you like your room?" Kamejah asked after giving me a tour. I felt like a tourist and she was my chaperone.

"Yes, I love it actually. I am so grateful for your kindness cousin Kamejah."

"Call me Kam, everyone calls me that. Go ahead and unpack your things. I will be in my room if you need me."

"Ok, I will do just that." Man was I humble; I use to be very sharp tongue with mother, now I am bloody near kissing Kam's ass.

"Oh, I do have a few rules." Her tone changed a bit.

"Announce yourself before coming in the kitchen from the basement. There are times I have guest or might be dressed inappropriately. That's one; secondly I will allow you to have male friends, or better yet one. I am not running an easy come in and out heat supplies services in this house." "I will comply Kam. I don't have a boyfriend so there will not be any need to worry about that."

Kam left me in the kitchen eating a fruit salad. What a difference a day makes, here I thought Jay's house was my only resort, 24 hours later I am staying with family. Real nice, upscale family: no more rats, roaches, sheet rock banging, loud arguments from neighbors, people selling dope in the hallway, pissing elevators, and thugs checking out my assets.

After eating my fruit salad, I unpacked, showered and hit the sheets. This queen sized bed was ten times more comfortable than my old bed. I was out for the count, like when Mike Tyson knocked out his opponents for the win in the first round.

"Hmmm, oh yes baby….oh, oh." I was suddenly awoken by a familiar sound Pablo had me making. Remember I told you Kam's bedroom was right above mine, go figure. Whatever, whosoever was giving it to her, must have been good, for she moaned and groaned, the bed foot and head banged against the sheet rock wall, thought I escaped all this from Brooklyn. Guess sex is standard wherever you go.

Homeboy was really laying his pipes down! I was jealous for a quick second, shoot, I cannot front I missed sex. I used to getting laid almost every night for years now. In the beginning of my relationship with Pablo it was exciting, but as I grew old and tired of him, so did the bedroom action. It was more of a machine performance, robotic, rubbery lame ducky. Too many rhyme words right? Laugh that was the intent here, laughter is good for the soul.

"Who is your Daddy?" Kam's rodeo was asking in control mode as he hammered the life out that bed and I can imagine her sweet French roll too. I am being polite; it's my cousin I am describing here. Funny, Pablo was my Daddy damn near every night. Sometimes he was my doctor, teacher with his long measuring ruler. However, I loved when we played dining out or more like eating out. I was the waitress and he was the dinner guest sampling the sweet desert from my serving, silk, laced or cotton tray.

"Spank that ass Daddy, I was a naughty girl." That man was playing with his hands, or whatever he was using. My cousin sounded as though thrills were running through her body. Hope this performance doesn't take place each and every night; these walls are too thin for my good. Day light where are you? This role play is deafening my ears, not to mention tingles my center piece, although I said I was taking a break, however, hearing a good session from other folks entices one's appetite and causes juices to escape. I know what will do the trick, an iPod; playing music will lessen her noise effect.

The morning after the role play in the hay, man Kam and her man finished their spanking, humping session around 3AM. *Oh what a night, late December back in 1963*, was the actual lyrics from the 70's song right; in this case, it was more like, *Oh what a night, rocking his beat quite pass three...*

Well I got dressed, and yes in something red, a red tank top actually tight blue jeans and a 2 inch red flip flop. Wearing red was like second nature. I really didn't put much thought into it. As I was about to walk up the stairs leading to the kitchen, I heard voices from the dining area.

"Oh babes, stop! Remember my cousin is staying downstairs and she might be up for breakfast shortly."

Kam was actually remembering I was here; last night was a complete different case for sure her memory must have escaped her for couple great sweltering hours.

"How long will she be staying?" The curious male voice asked.

"I told her 3 months, however if she is good it won't be a problem for her to stay longer. Why do you ask?"

"I am use to having you anywhere in this house, she is cramping my style." The mystery guy answered. If you ask me he is a selfish beast.

"Well I guess this means, I can spend more time at your place, right?"

"Whatever your wishes are babes." This guy is a player, he cannot answer Kam's question with a direct yes. I can tell he is up to no good. Guess my cousin needs to do some trading. I can tell her the key things to listen, look, and expect in general from a man, while she gives me business skills, lodging and a job. I didn't bother going in the kitchen, besides I had money to buy food from Auntie-B's restaurant which was conveniently minutes away from Kam's shop.

Kam, had me doing more inventory, she said a good shampoo girl must know all the products in order to up sell services, for instance treatments, coloring and extensions. I had a full head of hair and it was very long and thick. I always wear it in ponytails, or buns. Kam said that will have to change. I need to look the part; my hair must be different at least twice each week. Kam is a successful business woman, so she leads and I will follow. The weirdest thing though, the entire day I pictured her doing the naughty with her man; how different she acted now in the salon, but last night she was a porn star. Oh my goodness I am laughing on the inside.

Three more days, before I head back to Brooklyn to check on King Phil and my cakes. I indirectly asked Kam how much cash it takes to open a salon; her estimate was pretty feasible, 30 cakes. So I figured if King Phil gave me 15 in the next couple of days, I will damn near be half way there, plus with what I had in the bank, I am good money. Word!

"What your brain studying Keke?" Kam was smiling at me day dreaming. It was a Wednesday and the shop was slow. "Just life and learning as much as I can from you and be very good at this business of hair care."

"Nice I like that, in two weeks I will buy a mannequin for you to practice chemicals, cutting and styling within a month or so you will be almost a pro. I really need you to focus on the craft and not the money right now, which will come in time. The better you are at this craft, is the better your financial outlook will be." Kam was nice, I am feeling her and she is being genuine, taking me seriously; never had anyone treating me like this!

Chapter 5
The White House

Quick thinking hustle, that's my mother's temperament, Jay texted me a message, guess she realized I wasn't going to call her anytime soon. Anyhow mother rented my room the day after I left. Good for her, hope it works out beautifully, like when *'Harry met Sally'*. A young man at that for a tenant sound kind of suspicious to me, to rent my room so quickly and to a young male at that, moms is a trip like that movie. Remember that hit song and academy award winning film 'Hustle and Flow'?

You know it's hard out here for a pimp. When he tryin' to get the money for the rent. Makes good ringtone for her cell phone, so sad she didn't have the right hustle game like Auntie-B and her children.

"Where are you?" Roberta's voice on the end of the phone asked.

"Living in heaven, glad to be out from that hello hole, thanks for asking." I replied very sharply.
"Happy to know you are in heaven, hope all good things remain the same for you."

"I will try my best, let's change the subject. How are my little ones?" I loved those kids, the sound of their voices calling me Titi or Tia, melts my heart.

"They are doing good, come visit anytime you feel the need to. I know you want out from the projects mentality, but if you ever need a place *mi casa es su casa*." Roberta was fishing for information, to rat to mother dearest. In time they will

37

know I am with Auntie-B and her clan. I prefer them to hear it from the vines.

"Don't count on it sistah dear, don't." There was no point in continuing this telephone conversation, so we ended it with no resolve that she was looking for; well just that I am not swimming among the fishes under the Brooklyn Bridge.

It was now Thursday, the shop's busier than yesterday. Roberta called me on my thirty minute lunch break, messing up my flow. Anyway I made $40 dollars in tips already, although I was excited my mind was still on my 10 cakes with King Phil. Five stars would be this Saturday and there was no way Kam is going to be happy with me not being around on the busiest hair salon day. The only option I have is to give him an extra day, yeah Sunday; Kam's is closed on Sundays.

"Keke, you really don't have a boyfriend?" Kam asked in a very disbelieving voice.

"I don't Kam, not really focused on men."

"So what are you focused on, women?" she asked with major attitude, then laughed out.

"Comical Kam, I am going to call you from now on. Relationship is the least of my worries." I felt the rudeness about to surface, but then that voice spoke reminding me that I live with this woman who is making silly gestures. A war of words wouldn't do me any good and I have to keep this in mind moving forward.

What's that feeling? Oh my cell phone vibrating, I am not use to it on vibrate. I was told to do so, as a means to not get distracted as I am on the job training and not to mention my hands in water constantly. It was a text message from King Phil. "Change of plans, blue sky over shadows green. This Sunday will meet you with Dyer needs." Not sure why I am surprised, King Phil knew exactly where I am living! Now how on earth will I meet him on Dyer after telling Kam I don't have a boyfriend? This guy Phil was no joke, this message right here, has me shuck.

"Keke, Keke!" Kam yelled to get my attention. My thoughts were gone forward to Sunday, what on earth could have taken place since I left Brooklyn on Monday? I was a complete zombie, I understood Phil's text message clearly, and how do I pull this Bronx meeting off without a glitch?

"Yes Kam." I answered after she tapped me on the shoulders.

"You better come down to earth, all day you in space as though you carrying the world on your shoulders. Whatever it is, put it aside for now and we can talk about it when we get home later."

Kam is like a big sister, mother and cousin all wrapped in one beautiful body. A body and brains I admire, I really need to not only learn the hair business from her but most importantly how she thinks and what makes her who she is.

The next two days need to hurry up and be here already, shoot, I am anxious to know what on God's green earth happened to my cakes. That Thursday night Kam's lover never came over and the house was completely quiet, which was great for me. Needed that in order to think and process Phil's text. I don't have a body in Brooklyn to even ask what went down. I felt like my streets credibility was losing grounds here, it's a golden rule to always have a pair of eyes behind you. No matter where you move to, your last place of rest or dwelling should have a look out or trustworthy source. Once you leave a neighborhood, folks tend to the think you are making major money and you leaving them behind. Not knowing the facts about your move will lead to gossip and gossip brings jealousy which can lead to becoming a marked target. Oh yeah I forgot Kam wanted to talk about my absentmindedness at the shop today. I basically avoided her by pretending to be sick.

It felt as though I was on pins and needles, late Saturday night I talked with Kam for a second. Told her a friend will be stopping by from Brooklyn. I had to for the most part, wasn't sure what Phil had in mind. It was obvious he knew where I lived based on his text message.

'I am outside' Phil's text message read, no code just direct to the point. It was around 11am. I walked out as though I had garbage to put on the curb. With my cell phone in one hand, Phil text me his location. He was in an old silver Toyota Corolla, I replied to his message to meet me at Golden Patties which was around the corner from Kam's house. I walked into Golden Patties, ordered a drink and a juicy beef patty, got into his car. Reason why I acted as such? A great number of cabbies are on that block, so if I was being watched, Phil's car would be mistaken for another cabby. I had to take control of this meeting. Phil had to know he wasn't the only smart one here.

"Lady Red, I love your new location."

"Great for you, guess stalking is another trait you have besides being a baker of green or white products."

"That's why I am the King. I know everything about everyone who is important to me."

"Ok Phil, let's cut out the small talk and get down to business. Show me the money."

"Hold on I got it but first we are going for a ride, a change of scenery."

"Why? This is a quick 1, 2, 3 transactions, I don't need to see no change in scenery or whatever you have up your sleeves. Besides my cousin thinks I will back in a few. Hope this isn't a long ass ride out to Timbuctoo?"

"Cousin, huh or your man you living with?" He asked.

"What is it to you Phil, are you trying to be my man, my daddy or big brother? No, don't even bother answering, for you will never fit any of those category."

"Relax I am taking you to a place where no one else has been, it's one of my private spots."

"Yeah right, a place where you take your women for physical work out…spear me the secrecy, just give me my money." I was scared out my panties but I was from the streets so I had to play tough, damn no one from my family knew what I was up to. Phil could easily kill me and bury my body in some woods up in Mount Vernon.

We drove for about 45 minutes in silence, my body was at ease on the outside but inside I was petrified. I barely knew Phil, just saw him in the streets thought all he knew was Brooklyn and didn't get out much. For one of the streets rule is, a King never leaves his home ground, unless there is a turf war, or constant police raids. Phil runs the 90's and leaving solo without a solider to the Bronx was like asking to be killed. I mean I wasn't one of his chicken head females he sleeps with, so there has to be a valid reason.

"We are almost to the house; would you like some take out from one of my favorite Italian restaurant?" He asked politely.

"No I am not hungry, whose house are you taking me to Phil?" I asked with a slight anxiety in my voice. Being out of my element is never good for a girl like me.

"My house, what are you afraid of? It's kind of late to be worried about what's next, don't you think?"

I shook my head in agreement, he was right. I just had to go along with the program. If it meant driving all the way out to Long Island, then let the game begin. We pulled up to a white brick two storey house, the driveway was arched shaped and about a block long in length before reaching the front door. Lawn freshly mowed. God damn Phil was living a double life, but then again, he was making real paper in the hood. King Phil is the heaviest dealer in Brooklyn, so I shouldn't be surprised at all.

"Lovely view right Keke? Wait until you see the inside, especially my bedroom."

"The only thing I am thrilled to see is 15 thousand Benjamin Franklyn green paper with legitimate serial numbers." I had to let him know, I wasn't all impressed with his mini-mansion. I wasn't about to stroke him, or his ego.

Walking a few feet behind him, I entered his all white interior house. We stood out like two black spots in a glass of milk. Ok, let me rephrase, like two Oreo cookies in a class of milk. His house was spotless; smelling like garden fresh flowers was sprinkled throughout the house. I wonder who cleans, or even cooks here. Knowing this Jamaican freak, since it's been said most of them are. He might have a few hidden cameras, hope he doesn't plan to seduce me and record it for safe keeping. Who really knows if he would blackmail me, giving his torrid lifestyle?

"Have a seat in the kitchen. I will be right with you." I sat on a white stool at a mini-bar set up he had in the kitchen. This stool was fancy and apparently expensive; it stood on four legs each carved in the shape of a Lion's paw for great emphasis on strength. Bringing my focus back to what's at hand, I realized he disappeared into the thin white clouds so to speak. I could get use to coming out here for a ride now and then. Phil was a real King; this house solidifies that.

"Let's do business now Phil, come on now the suspense is killing me." I said as soon as he appeared in the kitchen in a change of clothes. He had on a white Polo cotton shorts and a sleeveless black cotton T-Shirt that showcased his ripped muscles. There was something different about him though, real different, I just couldn't quite put my finger on it. Besides I am here for my money and not to figure out who this mystery man is.

He walks over to the counter, pulls open a draw takes out a large white laundry bag. "Here are your cakes Keke; $20,000 to be exact."

"$20,000, why I thought we agreed on 15 stacks?" I asked a bit puzzled.

"True, but I have something in mind that will make you earn 100 times that amount in 2 months, well that's if you are interested."

I paused, lost for words and however watched him as he laid the stacks in front of me. I sat in disbelief, never have I done this type of transaction. Having my money was one thing but being all the way out here and not having another means besides Phil to get back to Bronx, I felt like trapped mice. Using rat wouldn't be appropriate given our lifestyle, for rats are known informants, whose life span is usually short-lived.

"Alright, let me hear what you have in mind Phil. One thing I know for sure, in this game there is no guarantee, so don't try giving me baloney, this plan better not be a huge balloon."

"I swear you women have one thing in common, when talking was giving away you all stood in front of the line and got it all." Phil was getting annoyed with me and his tone changed, like a warning sign for me to shut the hell up!

"Now let me continue, Keke it's no secret I like you and recognize that you don't have anyone to back you in the streets. Let me be the one to take care of your needs."

He stopped, waiting for me to say something or deeply look into his eyes but I didn't. Instead I sunk my stare firmly on the flooring, yes the all-white immaculate floor we both stood on. Eye contact can be a dead on means of manipulation but I learned well from my brother. Lack of eye contact and a giving off a deep thinking attitude, gives both parties mixed and unreadable signals.

"Okay the silent treatment, I get it. Your offer of $5000 from the 20 is not a major deal for me, as you can see around here is of the finest quality and worth a minimum of 1million cakes easily."

"So now my money is small fries and cheap fish cakes? What a way to put a woman down, that you so openly like and care for."

"Keke, I want you to think big and someday own a house like this, stand on your feet and not lay on your back for a dime."

How funny was his statement from a man who clearly wants to have sex with me, hence the reason he took me all the way to Lynbrook Long Island just to give me money and a pep business talk. Come on, who is he fooling?

"Forget it Keke, just take the money and do you. I don't have time for kindergarten kids." He said and then walked out the kitchen, disappearing for 15 minutes. Meanwhile I was counting each bill to be sure I wasn't being double crossed by Phil.

"It's all there Keke, no need to double check but here open this box I got you something special."

Phil handed me a white gift box and of course wrapped with a gold and white ribbon. I swear this man was obsessed with white, or am I paranoid?

"Go ahead open it, don't be scared." After putting the money back into the bag, I opened his gift box. Wow! Another lame attempt to get me into bed, Phil bought me a red Victoria Secret lingerie. Believe me this one was exclusively from the catalogue, I know because I shopped in the store at least twice per month and never saw this design. This lingerie was definitely ordered.

"Nice color Phil, but why not white like everything else in this house?"

"Girl all you wear is red; I've noticed you for a longtime Keke, a very longtime."

I love a man who pays attention; Phil was a mystery man to me, but he obviously knows plenty about me. I heard Jamaican men are rough in the bedroom and based on his rising buff in those white shorts, Phil would probably put me in the emergency room. After all I just had an abortion and my body needed to recoup from that procedure, or better yet I don't really want to be another drug dealer sex bunny, hell no, not again!

Reaching out for my hands to be one with his, without saying a word I went along with him for an official tour of this beautiful white house. How hilarious, I felt like the first black lady roaming through the irony of a white house.

Walking around upstairs, I was anxious to see if any of the rooms had a different color than white. Hey just a thought right? Why you may ask? I was just hoping there was an odd room; this pure white was becoming very boring.

"Welcome to my bedroom Keke, this room I want to make love to you someday."

"Why someday, why not now?" The horny freak jumped out asking, oh snap I was surprised I didn't tear his clothes off and ride him. Yes like a jockey until we both reach the finish line. Oh heavens, hear the Jamaica freaky side talking to my inner self. How foul inner words, lusting instead of letting him pursue me. I really was sizing him up, somebody pinch me please. I need to shake this off!

"From the looks of things Keke, you are not ready."

"What do you mean by that Phil?" I know I was sounding a little desperate, but when a man entices a woman to only turn her down. This dude playing some serious mind games.

"Look at your breast." He said pointing at my 34 cup twins. "I know that could only mean one of two things…" he couldn't bring himself to say what those things were, for he was right about one. My breast leaked thanks to aborting Pablo's baby. I didn't even realize it. I was so focused on the money and the anxiety of not knowing why he took me far away from the Bronx, must have worked up my hormones.

Chapter 6
The Feds Come Knocking

Back to business as usual, working at the salon and then going home, listening to my cousin mid-night porn sessions and me saving for a rainy day. My robotic life. Why? It's now 2 months since I'm living in the Bronx and I let Phil talk me into letting him flip $5000 for 3 months. Each Sunday he picks me up like clockwork and we drive to Long Island to his white mansion. To my surprise and to this very day, Phil has not made any attempts to have sex with me. He bought me that sexy Victoria's Secret and never asked about it again. I find this a little strange, as I have been told that Jamaican men are very controlling. If he was, Phil was using another means of controlling me, well what am I talking about, the money stupid. He was controlling me by having my initial money turn over each week. One thing he did each week on the island was a great deal of pep talk about life and what he wants from me. He wants me to live like a Queen, not a struggling tramp.

"Keke, are you going out today?" My cousin yelled from the top of the staircase. It was Sunday, and Phil cancelled our date, said something went down last night in the 90's and he had to stay put.

"No Kam. I am staying home and chill. Why?"

"Well I will be heading to New Jersey for the night, won't be back until mid-day tomorrow, so don't open the shop tomorrow take an extra day to relax."

Glory hallelujah, I am going to have this house to myself! What a treat, oh what a night it's going to be, my own piece of mind. You know what I am going to cook a nice meal, buy a pound cake, have grape nut ice cream, and red wine.

What a beautiful Sunday, nice cool weather. I have almost $100,000 stashed in my room. I am happy, feeling independent to some extent. Man I am going to enjoy and truly relax my overworked body. The only thing that bothered me is Phil. I wonder what could have gone wrong in Brooklyn last night. Hope not a bust and my money got tied up in a raid. Then again I had enough funds, so losing 20 cakes is minor. I am more concerned about Phil. I was developing feelings, yes I was like a horny male dog but I refused to throw myself at him, since he wasn't making any moves.

Perfect timing, Kam leaving me alone gives me time to watch my 50 inches TV in quietness. All week they have been promoting Reggae Singer/Songwriter Patra, her hit single 'Romantic Call' was blowing up the streets! Her colorful fashion was being copied by most yardies and even Yankees as well. However, her best trademark was her braids, yes them long ass braids that probably weighed a ton, if you bought human instead of synthetic. Well I wasn't into her fashion, only her music besides my hair was naturally long, curly and thick.

"What's cooking Shorty?" I asked myself out loud and just in case you readers are wondering, I made baked chicken quarts, potato salad, Spanish rice and fresh salad. Can I say it enough already, what a beautiful Sunday, and wonderful life!

***

There's nothing like a quiet, cozy, comfy bed, it's almost 10:30AM I am too lazy to make breakfast, not interested to call Phil, not interested in moving a muscle actually. Just want to lay in bed and chill, perhaps playing with myself, since Phil was treating me like a little sister these days.

Damn who the hell is ringing the doorbell so impatiently! "Coming, give me a second." I yelled from inside, as I walked up the stairs, passing the kitchen then the living room heading for the front door. A white, blue devilish eyed man stood on the landing.

It was UPS with a delivery for Kam. I quickly signed for it, closed the door and rested the package on the coffee table. Guess Kam wasn't expecting this; for she would have at the very least mentioned it or asked me to listen out for the bell.

Since I am up might as well I pour some corn flakes and have a bite to eat. Damn I was wet from thinking about Thick Phil, it's funny I went from calling him King Phil to Thick Phil, his imprint was blinding or distracting for lack of a better word. Wait who is at the door again? This time they were banging like we owe rent or the mortgage was overdue and coming to foreclose the property.

"Who is it?" I yelled standing four feet from the door. I wasn't expecting anyone, nor do I like opening the door to strangers, this was Kam's house not mine. I never had a visitor for the short time I was living here.

"Open the door, we are Federal Agents!"

Oh shit, think fast Keke, if my panties were wet before, now they are soaked with sweat instantly.

"What can I do for you? I asked as I gingerly opened the door. Never in my life had I any run in with the Police much less the Feds. The Feds don't knock unless they got some serious evidence.

Pointing his gun at me, the bowl of cereal fell out my left hand.

"Step away from the door, what's your name?" The white Italian officer asked.

"My name is Keisha Lopez." I answered like a two year old in fear of being spanked. I was a chicken. I was afraid of what was coming next. Shit I've only seen arrests on TV, never witnessed any dealers on the corner being locked up, just heard stories of what went down.

"She isn't the one we are looking for Charlie, but we have to take her in."

"I know Steve, she accepted the package." Charlie told his partner and by this there were 5 black SUV parked in the drive way, surrounding the house as if I was a mobster. Agents were coming out of each vehicle like a trail of army ants, crawling towards food.

"Keisha Lopez, you are under arrest for accepting the delivery of illegal drugs. A female officer will escort you inside to change your clothes." Charlie read me my rights, as the tears ran down my face. What on earth have I gotten myself into?

It was cloudy, I couldn't think, nor do I dear to speak as this frail looking white female officer escort me to my room and watched me change, she even had me squat and cough. Making sure I wasn't hiding coke in my vagina. Can you imagine my fear, all I did was cry, cry like I lost the only thing I had in my life and in this case it would be my freedom.

When I walked up stairs into the living room, the agents were searching, turning over the cushions, papers, draws, they had a search warrant. The package I signed for had something looking like a 5lb bag of Domino Sugar, wrapped in duct tape.

"This is what you signed for Ms. Lopez, 10lbs of pure cocaine, were you aware of this package?"

"No officer, no." My cousin's name and shop information was on it, now looking back, what on earth was Kam into? Did that bitch set me up? She conveniently left yesterday and took today off and to make it worst, instructed me not to open the shop. Now I am feeling like a mouse in a trap, forget about being in Phil's house for the first time. That was different; I wasn't in handcuffs nor in a room filled with Federal Agents.

"Let's bag everything we find for evidence and yellow tape the house, no one enters after we leave the premises."

I kept quiet, as they drove me to Central Booking in Manhattan to be arraigned. I have no one to call for help, absolutely no one.

I was facing drug charges, alleged charges. I was booked and sent to Rikers Island, and was scheduled to return before the Judge in one week. I was in a green jump suit, blood shot red eyes, shit I was weak and out of my mind.

This process was humiliating, stripped searched, holding a mirror between my legs as I squat naked. The guards were ensuring I wasn't bringing in contraband. I shook my head as my hair hung loose. I lift up my breast, and they searched me like an animal. And smelled me like I was their supper, one guard said to another, "She's fresh meat, first timer, someone will break her in nicely." They both laughed at my fear for this place. Rikers Island had many stories, many horrid and disgusting stories. They served the new intakes sloppy imitation of Jamaican rice and peas with some fresh tasting pepper steak. I could poison snakes, and stone birds with this meal; when do you ever know of a meal being a threat to animals? Yeah right never, so why feed us this over processed cancer filled food?

"Now ladies, guess it is ok to address you inmates as such and with that I expect you to act accordingly! Do you hear me? No do you understand the words I speak?' The Supervisor for my unit yelled on the top of her lungs. Man these bitches had a four on four girl fight last night causing the entire unit to be on lock down. Shit I am here in a 16 by 8, with a cot, toilet and a sink to wash my Spanish mix breed ass. Hope the Supervisor letting us out for a few hours, interaction in jail helps with mental stability, yeah according to studies.

"I will say this only once, you will be free to come out and sit in the lounge area, watch television and play games if you so wish. However any interruption, loud talking of any sort, trust and believe I will lock this unit down for four days!" Superintendent Houston yelled again. God damn it, I swear she got her job title for being able to shout.

Freedom! I screamed on the inside, watching few hours of television and chatting up to some real gangster chicks. Oh please, freedom is getting the hell out of Rikers, plus my cousin being in the same unit. I may even start a fight myself, stomp her in the neck for setting me up like the way she did. A real coward.

As I sat on a hard plastic green chair, another cute Spanish inmate pulls her chair up next to mine trying to make small talk.

"So what are you in here for?" she asked.

"I was set up; some dumb drug shit these crackers trying to pin on me!"

"Drugs! Oh shit, that's baby time my nigga. I am looking at 25 to life! My man stole a brick from my apartment. I hunted him and his new bitch down for about a week and stabbed him five times in the neck. His new bitch was lucky I only scratched her face up a little." She recounted. She was shaking with anger, not even regretting what had happened.

"Damn, that's a tough case Ma, he deserved that shit though. I swear these dudes are grimy and cold"…before I could finish my sentence the siren sounds off. Looking behind me all I could see was a group of inmates kicking another helplessly on the floor. Within minutes the unit had guards with tear gas or whatever the hell they had to scare us to get the hell back into our individual cells.

Father God, where is the Shango when I need him? The thought ran through my mind as I hurried into my cell.

Damn near 48 hours after being in this unit, in walks my cousin Kam. I wanted to pounce on her, rip the weave tracks from the roots making her bleed, making her feel the fucked up pain I was feeling right this very minute.

Wide, I walked and kept my distance from her. She was the enemy as far as I was concerned. The perfect life, well yes I kept on saying I was living that way with Kam. Never judge a book by its cover is a true statement. I will never ever take it for granted.

"Keke, let me say something to you, please don't walk away." Kam had the nerve to whisper behind me as we stood in line for lunch.

"Cool, guess I don't have a choice but to hear you out." I wasn't particular to have her in my space if I could help it. But being locked up, there wasn't a place to run, to turn or even hide.

I got my tray, which had salty food, sugar filled jello and an orange. I traded my food for fruits. I don't care for the sloppy platter. I wasn't use to this; so many girls were in here like a revolving door. My head was screaming on the inside, the very same thing my brother didn't want for me happened. I lived in the hood for so long and never got in trouble, however the minute I thought I was out of the hood, this shit happens. Damn son, why the hell me, I hustle for Pablo and never got caught, yo my dude this shit is messes up! My internal thoughts were raging, ready to snap off Kam's head as she sits next to me.

"We getting you out Keke, don't worry about your court date next week, cuz."

"Why should I trust you Kam? Why? I feel as though you knew the package was coming and you jet to Jersey, leaving me to get knocked."

"No, Keke, that package was a set up. My lawyer is working on the details of the address, think about it, why the package had my house and shop address."

"Set up my ass!" I didn't believe one word she said.

"Keke you have all right to feel the way you do, but hear me out. Just before you came to the shop I had a girl working there name Sophia. She was dealing in the shop that's why I let her go. She had packages coming to the shop almost weekly. I confronted her; we had a big cuss out in the shop. Never in my wildest dream…"

"So you never saw this coming?" Kam was a real dumb chick, business smarts but street foolish.

"I know it sounds lame, but no, I never let my workers know where I lived."

"Well explain all the cash the agents found in the house Kam, give me some answers?" She held her head down; obviously she didn't know I was aware of the evidence.

"Don't bother trying, just get me out of here next week, work whatever miracle you can; just let me be free from this bullshit."

All week my unit was under lock down, some real bad ass young heads and a few old cats were in here acting the fool. Snitching over a small portion of dope two were able to smuggle in. One day two ladies took turns showering a weak fence, I heard they ate her pussy like savages. It was her first time and she couldn't control herself, her loud mouth screaming in ecstasy got them all caught. Rikers has zero tolerance for sexual engagement. I don't even want to talk about this anymore. I am here counting down the hours to my court time. In a few hours I will be standing before the judge. The routine to appear in court, is all who have a court date had to get up around 4 am, showered and go through a long lengthy counting process. Why? Other units also had inmates going to court, so as prevent any of us from escaping, we walked from one section to the next and then to the bus. Oh, as for the bus, shoot, the windows were frosted or tinted. We were indeed animals, forever in a cage until we either die inside or make it out somehow.

"Your Honor, the defense asks that you release Ms. Lopez on the basis of ROR being it's her first arrest, no priors, no sealed records. The defendant was staying at the house in question for only 2 months and had no prior knowledge to her family member's operations." My female public defender was sharp, practically begging for me. I like her I really do.

"After reviewing the arresting officer's report, your defense is confirmed as such. I will release the defendant in the care of her mother in Brooklyn."

Thank God my mother came through for me; she was my only hope, my only means to freedom.

Chapter 7
Hear My Cry Oh Lord

The Lord is my Shepherd, I shall not want…the 23rd Psalm of David. Mother had me read it religiously each day since I came home from Rikers. She was petrified, she said. Guess she bought a Webster's dictionary, because I don't remember her ever using the word petrified.

"Keke, I went to your Orisha Deity Shango and made an offering to get you home free and free of all the charges. The Orishas found favor and granted my prayers."

"I hear you mother, so what's next? What does the Orishas expect from me? I don't have a full understanding of this religious belief; you've kept the secrets to yourself all these years."

"Next week the Baba wants you to come and spend a week, fast and pray and renew your strength under Shango. So whatever money you have prepare to spend some of it and gather the things he needs to perform the ritual."

I felt like I was involved in Voodoo, some high science witchcraft. Whatever it was my mother believed in it wholeheartedly, so far they have never failed her or me. My thoughts were on Phil. He had some money for me and yet I cannot get in touch with him since that Saturday he cancelled our Sunday date.

Auntie B was at court when the Judge sent me home on ROR. She paid my cab fare and gave me $1000.00. She was very sad, Kam hadn't seen the Judge yet, she was facing serious Federal charges. Kam deceived the entire family. Her boyfriend, yes her porn star, rough neck bed room bully buck boyfriend was second in command in the Bronx. His street name was Screw-driver; he screwed everything in sight and screwed anyone who crossed the organization out of money. I learned some of their stories since I got out. Screw-driver was wanted for at least 10 counts of murder and attempted murder in other States. That girl Sophia was sleeping with Kam's man and all hell broke loose in the shop after she found out. But what I don't understand is why take him back, why have him at your house ramming and jamming you like a pot roast? Guess the money was good. She was laundering his money through the salon. I cannot judge her, remember I stayed with Pablo after he got that tramp pregnant, so I am no different from Kam.

King Phil, oh I wish I could get word to you. His phone was disconnected and his presence was missed in the streets. Word on the streets or the latest update is someone from the 90's violated a member from the 50's posse. And this lead to rehashing old beef and since more money was popping in the 90's like a thief in the night when the UC were off duty. They fired shots on a house that had both cash and dope. The soldiers on guard were young and fled; the men from the 50's helped themselves to millions. Don't ask me, I wasn't there and glad I wasn't on the block when it happened. Remember Jessica aka Jay, my so called friend with her 10 fingers Tommy boyfriend. I swear his days were numbered in the streets, now that I am back I hope someone buss a copper in his balls for being so crafty. Well yeah Jay, got wind I was back and gave me the rundown of who is missing and who is dead. I never asked about Phil but she volunteered that he was still running things from an undisclosed location. Phil ordered the men to move the other store houses to Canarsie, parts of East New York and Brownsville.

If you should ask me, Phil had a snitch in his organization, because a real drug lord, keep things under wraps. Why on earth Jay knows all these details? I wonder if Tommy was working for them under the quiet, or spied for the men from the 50's. It's a known fact his step father owns a business on 52nd. The 90's checked him out and gave him the green light to live here, they knew he was a regular pick pocket tag runner on Pitkin Avenue. Petty thief, small fries, usually ends up dead on the side of the streets anyways, so he wasn't a threat to Phil's crew.

Life, as I see it has ups and down. I fell into a pit hole, a hole where my stash was lower than the amount I left Brooklyn with couple months ago. I have grown to like Phil, the past months with him opened my eyes to a man, a real man who has something of quality to offer a woman. Yes he pushed drugs in the streets, but the things he taught me about life and to survive with my head high on great possibilities and not on coke or looking for the perfect Suga daddy to support me.

"B, get your own, a real man loves a woman who can handle her shit." I remember him saying, in his thick Jamaican sexy voice one Sunday afternoon. I rubbed his back as he spoke to me that day and now and then rest my head on his shoulders. Phil never reciprocate any close feelings, he sat and talked. Maybe I was too young for him? He obviously knew I had an abortion and thought something about me he refused to share, and that was having me in suspense as my body parts grew fund of him. Phil was beginning to control me without even acting like an iron fist leader, he captivated my mind; my attention was set on him each Sunday we met. During the week while working at the shop, I would silently day dream of him probably laying a kiss on my lips, or even fingering me, God damn it I sure was feeling him.

Raymond, my dearest brother sent a letter while I was locked up for a week. I read the letter at least 5 times last night, he was disappointed. In his letter he said he asked God to send an Angel to watch over me, to guide me from now on, since he couldn't do a good job himself. I woke up feeling heavy in my heart, for my heart was missing two men, Raymond and Phil.

While standing at the window, overlooking a scheme of brick house tops, seeing guys on the roof, doing God knows what. You know how they like to have meetings on roof, or hide stash or even throw snitches off the ledge of roofs. If you ever lived in any hood, Italian, Black, Spanish, African or Asian, there was zero tolerance for rats. A real man or woman never gives up information to any authorities! There was no grey area, absolutely none about this.

I must have been deep in thoughts and didn't notice a pigeon was steering at me, a white one at that. I looked back and noticed a red string of cloth tied to his right foot. That sure got my attention, what was this about, the pigeon then suddenly flew off the window ledge. He did the same thing three times and by this it was obvious he was a messenger. Strange enough, red was my color and white was Phil's and that's when it dawned on me. Phil had shared a parable, that the number 3 meant 3 steps down, and since I was on the 3rd floor this could only mean I needed to go to the basement. But no one is allowed down there but the Super, for that's his dwelling place. The

Super, who had us calling him Johnny Bigz, had the entrance to the basement air tight. Gossip mill claims he was dealing underground passage for whenever the UC had a raid, soldiers could disappear from building to building underground, like what the slaves did from the South. Well I don't know and never investigated this alleged operations. I like to mind my business. I just listen to information for future use, for being informed was key importance for anyone to survive in any situation, especially in the streets.

I changed my clothes in a flash and calmly left my apartment, mother was still sleeping and there was no need to wake her. The lobby was quiet, no foot traffic or nosy peep hole on lookers. I stood at the door leading down the basement. There was something I noticed, yeah a strange white rectangular strip that I only saw at Phil's. You know those things the Jews have on their door frame before they enter a room they would kiss and touch it. To my surprise the door was open behind a fenced grill that the Super put up himself, this mechanism allowed him to see you, but you couldn't see him. If you should ask me the man was a real caveman, who protected his territory by all means.

Walking down the stairs, that was poorly lit, I watched each step carefully, making sure my feet was firm and they were able to hold my weight. Very spooky but there was another door, a mahogany wood fancy door that had no handle and could only be opened from the inside. So I knocked three times, then waited and waited till I heard the lock turn slowly. The Super let me in, not saying much he pointed to another door, which meant I must enter and be quiet. He then walked quietly up the stairs and locked me and my unknown surprised guest in the basement. I was a brave bitch, to enter into this room, not knowing who the hell I was meeting, although my gut tells me it's my man Phil, I just had a feeling. After standing in this well-furnished dark room, no windows, just an orange bulb, orange walls and ceramic hard tiles; shit this room could make anyone dizzy, like a disco room. I suddenly felt a pair of eyes on my back, or even my curvy backside.

"Keke." His soft, sexy voice said.

"Phil, is that you?" I asked like a real clown, knowing very well it's him. Phil scared me. I was asking myself where on earth he appeared from. Maybe he was hiding behind one of the furniture.

I turned around, and it was him all 6'2 of him. I ran to him hugging him and of course he didn't hug me back. What's the use in showing him any love, he was hard, I mean his feelings towards me or showing some affection was so hard.

"Where have you been Phil?" I asked as I let go and placed both my hands on my hips, talking to him like a wife demanding answers.

"I have been here, just couldn't leave. I heard what happened to you in the Bronx. Are you okay?" He looked me dead in the eyes, as if he was searching for something more than words from my lips. He was making sure I wasn't broken, or emotionally scarred.

"I am fine. The charges were dropped and I am free to start over again. However I need a better plan and plan where I am living on my own and working legitimately."

"How much did you lose?" He asked.

"Close to $100,000 and I am presently nursing $8000 in the bank." The Feds eventually released the hold on my bank account.

"Baby girl." He whispered in my ears. "I have some money for you, not much but enough to get you on your own and away from here."

"Phil are you ordering me to leave?"

"Yes, Keke. I strongly think you should, it will become crazier around here and I may have to give up my holdings in the hood. I lost big money, and all wasn't mine to begin with. I won't feed you much information and then you won't become a liability." He partially explained.

"Does this mean I will never see you after today Phil?" I felt my eyes swelling with tears. Oh shit tough girls don't cry in front of a dude; especially 'The Don'.

For the first time I felt Phil touch me, really touch me with affection. He grabbed my waist and planted a kiss, a kiss I was longing for.

"Phil, I think I love you." I softly spoke in his ears as we embraced.

"Think? You are in love with me Keke, for some time now, you just didn't realize it." Leave it to him to show off his confidence. I tell you Jamaican men have a reputation of being a big shot and hardly wanting to express love for their woman.

I couldn't believe the words came out but they did. "Phil, we have the furniture, they might not be white but they function just the same. Make love to me, for the first or as things look for the last." He held me close, kissed my neck, my breast and then slowly undressed me. Phil was gentle; it was as though he wanted to remember this day minute by minute.

After Phil undressed me, yes like a grown man unwraps a Christmas or birthday gift, slowly with drooling eyes and watering lips; Phil was a mess, a thirsty mess. I took him by his hand and walked over to a double sized bed. This room was huge. The bed had dark blue sheets, with about 4 flushed king sized pillows. I lay on the bed naked feeling excited, not knowing how he's going to feel inside me. What his entry will be like, I hope he doesn't tear me, Jamaican men are notorious for being large in size and rough in the bed but overall sweet like sugar cane once they are satisfied.

"Are you nervous?" He asked. I tell you Phil was older. I would say at least 15 years and with years of experience. For I didn't even realize my anxiety was showing so clearly, it's not like I'm a Saint.

"No, I am fine I believe this is long overdue." I answered him with sudden rushed feelings. I was like a school girl being plucked for the first time. Wet, moist, and ready at all the appropriate places.

To be very honest I was expecting a donkey-kong. However Phil had an elephant man. I was up for the challenge. Dear Jesus will I be able to handle this ride?

The further he entered, inch by inch my juices ran down his girth. I felt like a virgin and like a can opener Phil's rocket opened me up really wide. With all that, Phil was slow, tender; he wasn't hurried and wreck-less as if he was riding a wild horse. I allowed him to take charge, with each position he asked if I was ok, if I was in too much pain he would stop. He wasn't a punk. I could tell he valued me, and I him.

Chapter 8
Child's Play

Mother's 60th birthday was only 4 days away, so Roberta and I decided to host a party in Brooklyn. It was hectic, planning, preparing and organizing each detail needed for this to be a memorable one for mother. We haven't given her a party going on 5 plus years, she said not having all her children around was depressing; so we decided to honor her wishes.

However this year, Roberta insisted and convinced mother she needed to feel great about her life regardless of what has happened over the years.

"Keke how much money are you contributing to mother's party?" My annoying, cheap, slick-ass sister asked.

"I don't know. I don't have a job Roberta."

"Who are you kidding? You always got money, you are always lucky to have men giving you things."

"And as always Roberta, you have a problem with me and what men are doing for me. It's not my fault you don't know how to keep them! For the only way you know how to, is to get knocked up and put them on child support in order to get a penny!"

"You lucky I am not over there, be very happy we are on the phone or else I would knock your teeth back into last year, no wonder Pablo left your dumb ass for killing his baby. Who knows you're probably damaged and cannot conceive another baby; at least I have mine; you ain't got shit." Roberta was a meaner version of me when she got angry. She never liked hearing the truth about herself anyways. Roberta was a lazy enabling woman who expects men to throw money at her feet. She could never keep a job for long, when she does work, all she does is party, shops, and gives mother couple single dollar bills in comparison to the hundreds or few thousands I gave her. However kind this may appear, as soon as Roberta is broke, it's like mother had to give back the money, so in a nutshell she loaned mother a percentage of her pay check for a rainy day. Sorry ass!

I kissed my teeth in total disgust. I just went through a very horrible experience; I lost Phil to the streets and its war, and drug games. I am already giving mother money to help out around the house; thank God Phil gave me $25,000 the day we met in the basement. I wish she would come over and spank me, yeah she must think I am one of her young kids. I will mop her on the floor like a girl did to another at Rikers for talking filth.

Anyways it has been a week since Phil and I hooked up in the basement, each time I remember him I tear up a bit. You never how much you miss the water until the well dries up, mother and Auntie-B always said that phrase when giving advice about men and relationships. I guess it's a Jamaican thing; only old folks used parables to help mentally analyze people's behavior.

What's so funny is how the few times I see the Super he asked me if I was ok and needed anything. Guess Phil left orders for him to watch my back. Phil also ordered me to leave Brooklyn or relocate to another State. He said, "There is life outside of this concrete jungle Keke, think of the possibilities that lies ahead, you have enough money to start something new." His words after our second or third round, nearing his time to leave me, it was like a break up conversation between soon to be ex-lovers. "I might not be the ideal man for you Keke, you are young, smart, and only need a break. You honestly need a man who will respect and treat you accordingly. Not these nickel and dime hustlers in the streets. Not even me, certainly not me."

The way in which he spoke gave me goose bumps. It's as if Phil was hiding something, as if he had some deep dark secret. His life in the streets was like an open book, but his past, his core beginning in life was a mystery to me and perhaps to others as well. One thing for sure he cared for me. Phil truly cared and if I called it right, he had developed some level of intimate feelings as well.

***

My young nieces and nephews ran up and down the apartment, making noise, crying, fighting over toys, the TV and food. I tell you Roberta is doing a poor job at raising these bambinos. She too needed to be retrained or better yet trained to grow the hell up. That blasted whining, leaching, ambitionless, excuse for a woman. The cost for the party was close to $1,000; she only gave me $300. Then again I should be thankful she gave something, yeah right knowing her she will be leaving this house with more than $300 in food, liquor, and some of mother's birthday gifts. I tell you Roberta was a slick, poor excuse for a living being; always thinking people owes her something, or in her words, "The government, the world at that owe Black people and that's why Uncle Sam will feed and clothe my kids. The white man had us as slaves, took our land, so I am sitting my buttocks home and collecting." I guess that's all she learned in History class, the white owes her tons of money.

School wasn't my thing. I got caught up with Pablo and that was it. My ass skipped school and was hanging out with friends. Well I thought they were friends, when my brothers got busted they all slowly stopped coming around, some even avoided me when they saw me in the streets. The rule of conduct was, once you have money you're the man or woman; once you broke then you were the scorned trash on the sidewalk. I became the trash, but for Pablo who stood by me for the years he did; I was grateful he didn't look at me in this light. This taught me a lesson, a valuable one at that. I kept to myself, and learned to depend on me and the letters from my brother Raymond.

"Tete, I love you. Tete, tell Carlos to give me my Super hero." My favorite nephew Marcus said crying for his toys from his younger bullying brother Carlos.

Marcus was my child, if people asked me in the streets whenever I would walk him to the store, park and the mall. He was attached to me like special glue to wood. He was the first born, I had to babysit him a lot and it was no pressure or stress. Marcus was quiet and just loves to be hugged, and comforted. He wasn't active, he liked watching TV and play with his toys in peace.

"Carlos come here!" I yelled over the loud TV. "Give Marcus his toy now, you hear me!"

Carlos was spoiled and loved having his own way; taking any and everything in sight. I could tell what he will end up doing in life if his entitled mother doesn't break the tree from its young. Breaking the tree from its young was another phrase mother said to us many times as kids growing up, especially when we were disobedient. Clearly she said the phrase repeatedly, but didn't apply it. For if she had instilled some level of self-awareness and values we would not all be dysfunctional.

"What's going on here?" Miss Roberta came barging in the living room, demanding answers as to why I was yelling at her son.

"Carlos was being his usual self, selfish and stubborn." I told her in a very annoyed tone. I wasn't pleased with having her here for the weekend. Not only was she nosy, but likes to search around the house. I had my stash in my room. Well she tried me once and I cut her in the face.

When I was around 17, Pablo gave me $1500 for my birthday, told me to save it towards a car or whatever I wanted to get for my birthday. Of course I told mother, and she informed her big worthless daughter. So like every woman in the world we always have stash of cash somewhere in the house right. I left with Pablo to do a drop in Virginia, two days later when I returned $500 was missing. After I raised hell and turned the entire apartment into a garbage dump, I threw every living piece of furniture, books, and clothes onto the floor. I was like a raging animal. Mother came home and saw the condition of the apartment and we both started arguing. She was cussing in Jamaican and I was the same in Spanish.

"What the bloodclaat you doing Keke, you love sending my blood pressure up Pickney?" She said.

"Where's my money, where the bloodclaat back at you is my money." I asked her in a temper rage she had never seen from me. Mother immediately became nervous, practically shaking. I remember her calling Roberta to come over right away.

About 15 to 20 minutes later, Roberta dragged her lazy ass over to our apartment. She lived 3 blocks from us in the Bronx and yet it took her that long to get here.

"What the hell going on over here Keke, mother said you trying to fight her? Well I am here to slap your face back to infancy if you ever lay your hands on her!"
"Well I am not afraid of you miss bully, kindly tell your precious mother to hand over my money now bitch, or you and her will get it today!"

"Oh please, you are too mean Keke, I took that money. I borrowed it for the kids."

"What the shit you saying Roberta, why on earth would you do some dumb shit like that? This is the messed up shit I cannot take with your trifling ass. Who the hell told you to push them out if you cannot support them? Go walk the corner and sell your ass next time bitch. I want my money now!"

"Who you talking to Keke, who…" She ran up on me and slapped me in the face. I then pulled her by the hair. Roberta was bigger than me in body weight and size. Mother only screamed and shouted for us to stop. But neither of us listened, we pulled and fisted each other like two WWF Wrestlers.

At one point I felt my nose running, then blood was all over my lips, while Roberta had a few minor scratches. I was getting my ass whipped. Big bully made the mistake to stop to catch her breath. I walked away and unknown to her I held a small blade in my hands. Raymond taught me once, a true fighter never reveals his blade, he or she just uses it. I did just that and left a scar on her right jaw. Roberta yelled and screamed like a whaling pig in a slaughter house. We didn't talk to each other for about 2-3 years and she never gave me back my money. This was all good, considering her face was proof of her debt, a permanent scar for life sure worth more than $500, a matter of fact damn near priceless.

How comes I never went to jail for cutting that pig? Remember Pablo was in my life at this point in time and he rushed over the house after mother called him. There was a street doctor, he took care of street surgery. As you know the hospitals are required by law to report certain wounds and trust me Roberta and I stood to lose a lot if the cops had gotten involved.

So mother's birthday party was off to a good start, we had some new additions to the guest list. The usual list were the neighbors, a few co-workers, and us her immediate family. This time around mother invited her Orishas people from the Bronx. She had mentioned that the leader who did the offering on my behalf wanted to meet me, since I was taking so long to come to him, he made it his point of duty to show up.

The group consisted of more than 5 people, however only 5 showed up. Two were from Trinidad, one from Jamaica and the remaining two were Spanish from Puerto Rico. A very colorful bunch, both in culture and attire; they dressed like Africans. The three women wore wrapped skirts and lavish head ties. The material was very expensive. Mother whispered in my ear, while I poured drinks in plastic cups for them.

"So mother how comes I never see you dressed like them?"

"I do Keke, only when I go to the Bronx for meetings. I never liked traveling on the train in my pretty and very expensive African dresses."

"Oh it's as if you live a double life mother, a real double life after seeing these people."

"Hush your mouth gal and go serve the people them their drinks." She ordered me. She was the boss today, but any other day I would have challenged her.

We were having a great time, chatting about mother's life, her mishaps and fun time with the Orishas group from the Bronx. They shared information mother never shared with me, maybe Roberta knew since they talked on the phone constantly. As for me, no I was a loner always locked away thinking and making moves.

The leader of the group pulled me to the side and asked me a few questions. I was kind of hesitant but nonetheless polite, besides he was a guest in my house.

"Why are you afraid of us?" Brother DeJan Hamming asked.

"I am not afraid Brother DeJan. I've been very busy and need to find myself and not to mention a job."

"A job is the least of your worries young sister, you have something in the making; something that will forever be yours."

Was this man Jesus? Why is he speaking in parables? Guess this was his way of engaging in conversation, you know being optimistic and all.

"Come see me next week, no later than that. You have been running and no more of that." He was sounding very demanding, and yet trying to come across as being nice by smiling with a bright grin on his face. Who was he kidding, I don't take orders from strangers. I don't care if he offered up 10 horses and 25 lions for me to get out of Rikers. "Do you hear me Keke?" He was making sure I answered instead of nodding my head.

"Yes brother DeJan, I will." As soon as I answered him, his eyes balls began rolling; he was struggling to stand flat on his feet.

"Mother come here quickly! Something is wrong with Brother DeJan!"

"Oh! Oh no Keke, a manifestation is taking over his body, he'll be fine." She said as she and the other members walked into the kitchen. Roberta stayed in the living room with the remaining guests.

Mother went in the cupboard for ingredients and liquids, while the other members began singing. I couldn't understand what they were saying. I just looked on, and was in complete shock. I watched horror movies during Halloween and have seen actors pretend to have a demon pose their body, but never have I witnessed it up close and personal better yet in my kitchen.

Mother and the others called it manifestation. I say it's damn scary, like a force was fighting for control. I don't know of God functioning like this. Trust me Jay wanted to come and I am glad she didn't. Imagine her here witnessing this drama, only for it to make front page street news. I told her point blank no, when she invited herself. We only had a specific number of people and mother didn't want a crowd. She said nothing, but I could tell she was insulted. I didn't care, she was not a trustworthy person. I was slowly pulling away from her. The only time I needed her was when major events took place in the streets and I needed to be informed for my own benefit. Phil may no longer be in the picture to protect me but I needed to know my surroundings, as everyone knows I am indeed a loner.

"Pickney come!" Brother DeJan spoke in a very different voice, he acted differently. Before this so called manifestation took over his body he was very poised and calm. Now he was walking around impatiently, asking for ingredients to pour down his mouth, a cloth to wrap his head and demanded the women to sing. The manifestation sure wanted a whole lot; it's as if he wanted a party of his own or something.

"Who me?' I looked in mother's direction, asking her if he was talking to me. She motioned her head for me to come and address him.

"Pickney not coming to me why? I protect her all the time, me Shango!" He said to my mother as he beat his chest and mind you he was beating his chest very forceful. I was almost afraid he might have a heart attack.

I walked towards him slowly, looking directly in his eyes. I wasn't sure how to handle myself. The ladies instructed me to kneel down and acknowledge him and touch the floor with two fingers. I did as I was told. He, Shango then began anointing my head with oil, or something to that fact. It smelled real nice but was very greasy. Shango began to talk, saying things half ass, you know in parables like Jesus in the bible.

"You sleeping with the enemy, you will have twins, the truth no good news, no good."
I was glad when his manifestation left. He embarrassed me, he rubbed my belling every chance he could and talking about twins coming. The nerve, I need to read my bible to understand these spirit business.

Mother Orisha friends stay a few hours more than they had anticipated; we were all to be enjoying music like Calypso and Reggae not entertaining unknown spirits. I was anxious for the clan to leave my house.

Chapter 9
Hope Road

No woman no cry…I remember when we use to… Ever since my mother's birthday celebration, she has suddenly become very cultural and free spirited. Well the fact too, it was February and I believe there was a worldwide promotion of Bob Marley's music for two main reasons. One being it was Black History Month and secondly Bob's birthday was on the 6th. A sense of pride and accomplishment flooded the emotions of all Jamaicans around the world; my mother was a part of this wave heat.

"Keke, stop holding on to that sad face and come dance with me, this is your Jamaican culture. We grew up on Bob's music." My suddenly upbeat, happy go lucky mother ordered me, as I sat on the window sill in my room hoping Phil would send a pigeon like the last time.

It's been 5 weeks since I saw Phil, his touch felt as though we made love just hours ago. My body needed him, I missed his weekly lecture. I had obviously become addicted to him. Phil's personality, his swag and now his intimate touch has consumed my every thoughts and hopes for something more. These would have, could have, and should have ran rampant in my daily thoughts. I have never felt this way before; Pablo and I were young and didn't experience a mature responsible life. Phil offered something I never experienced. He offered hope, he was so encouraging. At first I thought it was a manipulation method to control my mind and body eventually. Players have so many different approaches and sometimes it's hard to recognize a real man from a player's weak line or intentions.

So I indulged my mother's order, got my butt up and joined her in the living room. I saw a side of her in that moment of enjoying the legend's songs of inspiration. It was as if she became a kid again. She showed me some moves, if you ask me mother was having a serious effective aerobic workout. When she took a break I started acting like a spoil brat.

"Mother my dearest person in the world, since you are in a good mood how about changing up the menu from the usual Thursday stew peas and rice. I am feeling for a nice cut of steak, baked potatoes, string beans, glazed carrots with my favorite homemade punch."

"Who is running this house? Me or you?" Yes the boss lady was back, she had been acting awfully nice since her birthday party. Brother DeJan's manifestation took her in a corner and whispered some good news; well she didn't bother sharing with me and Roberta.

"Woman such a mean thing to say to your youngest and forever caring daughter." Anyways I really didn't want it, I was just hoping for a slight change of routine. There's that word again, hope…not sure what came over me but of late I have become a hopeful softy.

Anyways back to reality, my stash was good but I was miserable. I've grown accustomed to working and collecting a paycheck at the end of each week, thanks to Kam. Speaking of the devil, I haven't bothered to follow up about her situation with the Feds. She and her boyfriend will have to figure that out. However it would be nice of me to reach out to Auntie-B, after all she was only trying to help me, and a matter of fact she did help me when I got out of Rikers.

My original idea of opening a salon was eating alive especially since Kam was locked up and Phil was missing in action. I have been trying to figure out who could I turn to for help; this stressful thinking was damaging my nerves and making my stomach nauseous one minute then craving another. A juicy piece of steak would fill the void, or take the edge off for couple hours or days, well temporarily.

"Keke come here a second!" Mother yelled from the kitchen. She was totally done and feeling tired from dancing to Bob.

"What do you want lady, you not cooking my order so stop bothering me!" I answered shouting from my bedroom.

"Big batty gal come here now and stop being fresh!" I dragged myself off my day dream bed and lazily walked to the kitchen.

"What do you want mother? This better be good, you've already disturbed me twice for the day and it's only 11AM."

"You living under my roof so I do as I please. If you want the steak run to meat shop and the Korean vegetable stand and buy the ingredients. I am in a loving mood, so you are luck today."

I stretched out my arms with a big grin on my face; mother kissed her teeth and rolled her eyes like a fresh pussy cat.

"Love you mother dearest, you are the BEST!" I said loudly, well I kind of sounded like an actress on Broadway.

"Whatever, girl with Jennifer Lopez' ass but not her money or a rich boyfriend; speaking of boyfriend when you going to call Pablo?"

"Mother why spoil a perfect day with a crappy question? Let me go get dressed and buy my steak, love you ma." I said as I kissed her cheeks and rubbed her natural black hair.

"He loves you Keke, Pablo just have a different way of showing it."

"Pablo loves every girl who opens up and play nice. I am done with that, done with the likes of him. I need a real man, not a beast, a man who cares and doesn't scare me into a corner and pounce on me like an animal backed in a corner." I gave my mother an earful and then some.

"You young people are very stubborn; well you've been sitting around the house like a depressed sick puppy in love." She said as I walked away, mother had to slap my big butt as per usual.

I left her in the kitchen preparing something, didn't care I just know I'm getting my steak later today. As for Pablo, who is the reason I haven't gone to the Bronx to see brother DeJan. I am truly afraid of running into him and his baby mother, or the new chick he's dating. Just don't want any drama; I will go see brother DeJan when I feel the time is right.

As I exited the meat shop, I almost bumped into a girl bending down fixing her boots.

"Sorry." I said to her.

"That's ok, my bad for standing in the door way." She answered without looking up.

"Wait Jay, is that you?" I asked as I recognized her voice.

"Keke! Hey love how you doing?" Jay asked as she stood upright facing me. She had on the latest True Religion navy blue jeans, a hot new pair of Timberland and a new burnt orange North Face bubble jacket. Her hair was dyed in streaks, burgundy and black.

"You are looking hot Jay, where you off to?"

"No place in particular, just felt like dressing fly. So what are you up to?"

"The usual, running grocery errands for mother dearest; you know she's happy to have me back home to cook for, as well as annoying me to shreds."

"Oh, that's mothers for you, as miserable as they get. Well have you at least heard the latest with the turf war?"

"No Jay, but I know you will fill me in." I said as we both burst out laughing.

Pulling me away from the concrete ears, to the curbside next to a garbage can, it was as I thought; she was a secret agent working for the Government.

"Girl there's a new leader running the 90's!" Jay was speaking softly.

"Oh really, what happened? I asked, not letting her know I had a connection with Phil.

"Phil disappeared and no one is sure where he might be…One of his baby mother's from 95th said he left for Jamaica two days ago."

"So is this change of leadership a good thing or can it be more dangerous for us innocent residents?"

"Well not sure, there's plenty being said and tons of guns and drug movement. The new leader they call him Trigger Slug 50, but for short he's being called Triggs50. I don't know how these street people come up with their politically correct terms and conditions." Jay explained.

"But what really happened? I never heard of a leader being changed without bloodshed in the streets." I was pressing for information without giving my hand away.

"Yes there was bloodshed, it just never made the news, some were more dumping bodies in places no one would find, you know the drill with our community." She whispered in my ears.

"Come with me to the Korean store, let's chill out at my house since you really don't have any major place going to." I insisted, for only one reason, to really listen and read through the talk and assess what went down. Phil was more than a leader to me; he was a man I had grown to have feelings for. I wasn't pleased to find out Phil has a ring of baby mothers under my nose actually within blocks of my house. Hey I knew he wasn't a Saint no matter how nice and polite a man is, he will always have a string of women or baby mothers. Why? It comes with the territory of being a very powerful man; besides this would give me the perfect opportunity to do my homework about Phil and this new leader. Well again hoping to hear accurate information from Jay, although most times she is.

Chapter 10
Eggs Well Done

"Sister Morgan, pass me the camphor and white oil quickly." Brother DeJan yelled as he was about to anoint my stomach. All this oil rub down was getting on my last nerves. I mean, I had to go to the Bronx like a thief in the night for this was a spiritual emergency.

How did I end up here? I went to bed around 9PM after eating mother's escovitched fish and festival, her usual Friday night special. I was tired from just laying around listening to mother and her stories. She talked about life in Jamaica, music, having me, loving me, to her daily soaps. My mind was all jumbled up with imaginations of different scenes and expectations as I tried to take some notes as she spoke.

The strangest thing happened, it was as though I was in a movie, but in actuality I was dreaming. In the dream I saw myself, dressed in red as usual. There was this black man who was also dressed in red, an African looking material.

"Count from here." He yelled at me and pointed at a set of small stones placed on a red and white Zebra print cloth; that gradually became larger as I counted higher in numbers.

"1, 2, 3, 4, 5, 6, 7, 8, 9." I counted as he instructed me to, however when I got to 9 there wasn't any more stone, a matter of fact that place on the cloth was empty but he was pointing to it. He then said, *"Open your right hand."* When I opened the palm of my hand, he placed an egg a white egg

84

to be correct. I was scared, never had a dream or woke up feeling like the earth shifted from under me.

I asked myself, why a mean looking man would talk, or even yell at me like that. I woke mother and she said nothing more than to get dressed; so I did and the next thing I knew we were on the FDR heading to the Bronx.

"Sister Morgan hurry nuh, move fast woman. This chile took too long to come now Shango have her tie up. What is to be will be Keke.. Many are called, however few are chosen." Brother DeJan rubbing my back, my belly and humming something weird, sister Morgan began catching some fever, or spirit. Man these Obeah people really working some magic with my body, thanks to mother hen. You should have seen brother DeJan head tied in green like those African women on 125th Street in Harlem. He had cow shells and beads around his neck. The pipe he was smoking had herbs in it, not marijuana, but some sweet herb.

Sister Morgan then wrapped my waist with a pink and blue material and instructed me to wear it for 9 days.

"Keke if he cannot get the mother then he will take the child." Brother DeJan said in a very disturbing tone, one that was serious as if to mean life or death. Whatever the case, these people need to talk straight, I do not understand one blasted thing they either saying or doing to me.

"Keke, when was your last monthly cycle?" Brother DeJan asked.

"Couple weeks ago." I answered not quite sure to be very honest. With all the worry and hoping about Phil I haven't been keeping track. "Why do you ask brother DeJan?"

"The egg and number 9 represents 9 months of pregnancy." He explained. I was in complete shock, but then again nothing beats a pregnancy test, so why should I believe these spiritual wonderers. Who are often times false like Miss Cleo with her thick fake crystal ball, scamming millions!

"Why are you so sure about this Brother DeJan?"

"Wisdom comes with years, knowledge and firsthand experience. You refuse to come and let Shango be your guardian now that you are of the age of consciousness. So now he wants your unborn child."

On our way back to Brooklyn, mother and I rode in silence. I reached for her hands and could feel how tense she was.

"Ma, what's wrong?" I asked her.

"I am worried for you Keke. I don't see any man around you, Pablo is gone and so who could be the father? Who Keke, who could do this to you? Did the guards rape you in Rikers? All sorts of things running in my mind right now Keke."

Resting my head on her shoulder, I rubbed my stomach, crying, for the first time I felt my mother's love. For some reason she's very loving these days.

"Ma don't worry I know who the father is, and no, absolutely nothing happened to me while at Rikers."

Tears ran like flood during a hurricane. Phil was gone, I had couple thousand dollars stashed, been depressed and not sure what direction my life was going. Having a fatherless child is not a fashion pocket book I wanted to wear in the hood. Another way of looking at my situation is that this baby could actually smoke Phil out from hiding in Jamaica or wherever he is. Who really knows what will happen next?

***

What happened next? Days after me finding out I was pregnant the way in which I did with them Shango people; was actually the lyrics from Bob Marley's' song *War in the East, war in the West everywhere is War, Me say War*.

Explosion in the streets, rattling and cracking of gunfire between NYPD and the men who ran the streets; the place was hot! The 90's was under serious curfew, a perimeter was set by the commissioner of police. From East New York Avenue to Kings High Way, that was one point of the boxed in, the other point ran from Remsen Avenue to Rockaway. No one could come in or out of these points unless they had valid identification, and mind you their ID's were checked for outstanding warrants and violations.

Some residents stayed home, didn't bother to roam the streets trying to find out who died from who remained living for the time being. The 90's was bleeding for certain, in whatever context we were all bleeding from this turf war.

"Hey Keke." Jay answered on the other line of my cell.

"What's going on with you?" I asked, knowing very well she was calling to give me body counts.

"Girl I am good, my boyfriend is here and he isn't going anywhere. Now you know a sister is happier than an Opera singer." Jay cracked up laughing as she was being very silly.

In my mind I was thinking, well at least she has a man; here I am pregnant for a man who is missing.

"Well base on how the word is in the streets, Keke, we ain't seen anything yet. Until Trigger Slug 50 is dead and EBones takes over from Phil, the streets will be in uproar. No one wants Trigger, word is and he's a cold blooded murderer." Jay's words sent chills down my spine. Who the hell is EBones? Afraid to ask her out loud, I mean it's not like she wasn't going to say. With Jay all you have to do is listen quietly, her mouth ran like a facet needing its washer replaced; CNN ain't got shit on her for sure.

"Hope you not going crazy with mother dukes, you two locked up and all thanks to this curfew nonsense! How are you passing time sis?" Jay asked with concern I guess.

"The only and best way I know how, eat, shit and then sleep. And there's the occasional television program during the day. The 90's is all over the local news stations, so our Tvs are stuck on cable."

"I hear that Keke. I hear that."

Why on earth should I tell Jay, I am a nervous wreck from both being pregnant and worrying about Phil's whereabouts? God damn these crazy soldiers of his, for starting a war that may not end soon.

EBones was short for Emmanuel Bones. He got his name because he was skinnier than an actual human skeletal in a coffin. I have never seen him, or maybe I did, but given the fact I never speak to them in the streets, I had no clue who was who. I knew Phil because he was always calling out to me for you know what. "Hey sexy, come chill with me tonight" was one of his teasing lines, that wasn't a pick up at all; well at least in my book. He was plain out right rude. So EBones, Trigger Slug 50, it didn't matter to me, I just wanted my Phil, my baby daddy to fly his body parts back from Jamaica. Well then again if he is there in the first place. Jay's gossip are usual on point so who really knows, but Jamaica I cannot picture Phil running there and leaving all this money, power and control behind. He was living the life in Long Island, yeah his double black and white life.

Chapter 11
The 90's Beat

Blame it on the rain, it began to pour down really heavy overnight preventing these hoodlums from firing shots, and us the residents subjected to loud never ending sirens.

The 90's brown stone brick houses mostly attached two family homes. A few big buildings, that housed low income families, mother and I lived in one. The private homes were mostly owned by West Indians; perhaps a few black Americans remained. When the dope, hit the streets, all them white folks sold out and ran like the world was coming to an end.

Summer time in Brooklyn is lively, girls walking around in all sorts of colorful attire, wearing several gold chains for whatever reason, looking to be a jump off for dudes who hollered as long as he had some money, she was down on the nearest mattress. Now and then I would sit on the stoop and watch these chicks play themselves, Summer time they would be with John, come Winter season they changed up the pace with Harry. Funny some girls weren't smart at all, they be shacking up with Harry during the Winter, got all cozy, right, then by Summer their hot gal fashion style all messed up because they got knocked up. A few pregos would show their faces, while the other kept their butts low key.

The ending of Summer is always great! Like really festive. The Caribbean Day Parade on Eastern Parkway, fever filled the streets with music and outrageous costumes. Calypso, Reggae, Dancehall, Steel Pan, and Haitian music filled the air. Tons of house parties, back yard bar-be-cues, and the occasional or traditional expected cuss out fist fight or just gun butting would take place.

The vibes was nice, a slight bit different from us Spanish folks in the Bronx. We had similar activities, with the exception of ending the Summer with a parade. Life, with its systematic rhythm, same beat just a different year.

Them Jamaicans, I mean the other part of my DNA, are fierce people. They ran the 90's like it was their backyard, drugs was like free reign. They were untouchable and unstoppable, some real rough and rugged men. Hey women too, they smiled with you but deep down they were hustling dope in their Salons or restaurants. Them cats knew how to make money honey. Talk about dressing, Naomi Campbell had nothing on these women, nor did Bill Cosby on the men. The fashion that rocked the streets were, Salt N'Peppa hair style, cut up jeans, policeman boots, midriffs tops and loud color makeup. For the men LL Cool J, Run D MC, kangol hats, rope chain, gold teeth and white Adidas.

Well the Jamaican in me was just like the real 100% blooded one. I dressed the part as them, my man Pablo's dollars was strong and I lived it up, back when I was with him.

One thing that's common at most New York City parks is the dealing of dope, weed and sex. I mean picture Lincoln Park off Buffalo and Eastern Parkway in the 80's and early 90's. Undercover cops worked round the clock trying to clean up that park. It took them years to finally get it together. Man it was like a rat infested joint, the more the cops arrested them bandits, the more they sprang up from nowhere. The 90's man, just say the 90's was a rough and rugged era.

Chapter 12
Mailbox Delivery

Acting like a new grandmother, this woman, yes this woman my darling mother is actually pampering me and making my sister Roberta jealous to the max. Life is funny before finding out I am pregnant, my entire focus was only on me and my goals. Brother Raymond hardly wrote; heard he was on constant lock down for bad behavior.

My brother only loses his cool when he feels completely threatened and fears his life. He's the last one to yell and step to any dude. Mind you he isn't a punk, never underestimate a silent river, it runs very deep.

"Ma did you check the mail box?" I yelled from my bedroom. Too lazy to roll my 4 month belly and big ass out the bed, much less to walk down the steps.

"No Keke, your legs still work right?" She answered.

"How mean Ma, not nice to talk to a pregnant lady." I responded jokingly. We were getting along very good these days; she is even suggesting names and acting as if I am only a surrogate.

"Ok mother I will go down in a few, besides I need some breathing exercise according to this book I am reading." I slowly got dressed, slipped on my Nine West penny loafers and snail walked to the mailbox.

Well the usual bills and junk mail. Looking through a handful of mails, the Super exited the door that leads to his domain. He watched me as if he never saw me before, shock painted his face seeing my 4 month belly.

"Hi, how are you?" He politely asked.

"I am ok, just taking it easy." I answered.

"Well if you need anything let me know, don't be afraid to ask alright?" He stated as his eyes focused on my belly. You could tell he wanted to ask, or he just automatically guessed I was pregnant for Phil. I wanted to ask him for Phil, but knew better. In the hood there are certain codes of conduct and I learned them from early; trust me I never break them. The Super is a stranger to me, since we never spoke until Phil signaled for me to meet in the basement.

"I will, I certainly will." The only answer I could give. Guess I am the only one living at my apartment, 9 out of these 10 envelopes had my name on it. A few were bills, baby coupons but there was one from the Bronx. I was afraid to open it, fearing the Feds might come pouncing on my door.

"Any mails for me Keke?" Mother asked.

"Yes your Sprint bill, the rest is mine."

"Now you see why I don't run and check that box? Only thing comes here for me are bills."

"Woman hush, be quiet I am reading a letter from Auntie-B."

"Oh yeah she wrote you, how nice of her to do so."

"Stop being condescending, Auntie-B is a very genuine person ma, very genuine and kindhearted." I stated. She's just being jealous, because Auntie-B never mailed her a card much less a note.

"So what is she saying?" Nosy mother hen inquired.

"Let me finish reading nuh man, cho rasta." Oh yeah I spoke patios every now and then.

Sitting around the kitchen table, reading my addressed letter; to summarize it all up Auntie-B was offering me the entire salon. Kam was sentenced to 5 years; a reduced sentence since it was her boyfriend they really wanted. He was serving more time, some serious hard time her letter stated. The Feds took the house, but the shop was in Auntie-B's name and after checking her paper work the Feds gave her the green light to reopen for business. Well after paying couple thousand dollars in fines; she was ready to walk away from the memory of Kam's demise. Her favorite granddaughter broke her heart, I could tell by this letter.

Keke I have enclosed a check for $3000 towards cosmetology school. I will move the equipment into storage and pay for it until you finish school and ready to open a shop whether here or in Brooklyn. Always remember that your Auntie-B loves you and will help you just I would my children. You deserve a great life, one that is free of major financial stress. Come and visit to keep me abreast of how things are going for you.

Love Auntie B.

Her words, strong meaningful and caring and I was sold on the idea of going to school, the only thing is I am pregnant,

4 months at that. This letter gave me hope, a sense of direction. I will write her back before the week ended but won't visit until after the baby is born.

"So secret Agent Keke, you telling your mother what your aunt said in the letter?"

"Obviously she doesn't know I am pregnant, she basically sent a check for me to enroll in cosmetology school."

"How much she send?" Ma asked. I know she was counting dollar signs in her head. My dear mother's brain only counts other people's money and you would think as her daughter I would at least know where her stash is. She was the secret agent, not me.

Chapter 13
Push, Pop, Surprise!

13 my lucky number, 13 more days before I pop this little boy out! Today's date was the 13th as well. Yes Phil and I are having a boy, come to think about it I am not even sure how many kids Phil has in total.

It's a beautiful Sunday Summer morning, curled up in bed with the air conditioner running, cooling my body heat and the heat from mother's kitchen. She was preparing a great deal of food for Brother DeJan's service this afternoon in Brooklyn. He was conducting a spiritual table of some sorts and mother's contribution is the food. She had from ackee and salt-fish to roast pork, chicken, goat and stew beef. This crazy lady was up since 4am cooking, smelling up the apartment building, smelling up my room and all. One thing for sure mother dukes can cook, she and Auntie-B have that in common and oh yeah a big backside too.

"Come on in Ma, I am sleepy make it quick." I said as she knocked softly on my room door.

"Some people are here to see you, please get dressed and come out to the living room and don't keep them waiting."

"Who are they?" I asked.

"Just hurry up and get dressed you will see." She answered.

I hate surprises, as I slowly got dressed, I racked my brain thinking who on earth could be in the living room on a Sunday morning at that? I don't keep many friends, in fact

I had none. Jay knew better than to show up at my house unannounced. I swear my room got smaller by the minute, shoot everywhere you look there were gifts for my son, towels, clothes, toys and even books as if he will be able to read.

Taking deep breaths before opening my room door to my Sunday morning blissful surprise, I rubbed my belly not feeling my baby move, guess he was sleeping.

"Good morning I said as soon as I stepped into the living room area.

"Good morning Keke" The two men said simultaneously, as if they were in church on the choir benches.

What on earth are Pablo and Brother DeJan doing here? I am not an addict needing an intervention. I sensed these two are going to send my blood pressure through the roof.

"To what pleasure do I owe this visit?" I asked, very confused. Mother exited the living room and headed towards her kitchen.

"Your mother loves you Keke and wants only the best for you given the family issues and struggles over the years." Brother DeJan put his words across nicely.

Trying his best to not look at me, Pablo was sitting in the coach nonchalant as if he was waiting on his queue to speak, as though they both rehearsed. I decided to sit next to Pablo instead of Brother DeJan. There was an awkward silence as I sat and got comfortable and for whatever the agenda these two had up their sleeves, me sitting next to Pablo put a smirk on Brother DeJan's face. I hit Pablo in his rib using my right elbow whispering in his ear.

"Pablo are you ok?" I asked, sensing this might be about him wanting to be a part of Brother DeJan's Orisha gathering 'cause I know for sure we weren't getting back together.

"Yes, I am. We are here to be a support to you and the baby." He answered. This crossword puzzle game these three were playing was now getting to be annoying and I don't do annoyance too well.

"Will either of you get to the point here!" I said raising my voice a bit.

"We all decided that since you don't have a father for your unborn child and Pablo is very much prepared to step to this role..."

"Wait a minute, what is it to you all? My unborn child has a father!" I yelled, although this tension wasn't good for my baby; again these three sent my autopilot temper from zero to eighty and believe me I was just getting warm.

"Pablo you of all people what you doing here? What role you want to play in my baby's life? After what you did to me! You got some balls coming up here, go father your chicken head baby mama drama in the Bronx and stay the hell out of my life!"

"Brother DeJan what did I tell you about her? She's not worth my time nor energy, just a pitiful character. I am sorry for the dude who knocked you up!" Pablo was spitting back fire.

"Well get out! And don't let me have to call the cops this Sunday morning!" I wasn't playing around with him.

"As for you Brother DeJan, stay out of my child's life! There is no need for you or nosy mother to concern yourselves; his father and I are fine and that's final!"

I got so upset, not even sure where the energy came from to lift my heavy behind off the couch and back into my room. I slammed the door, hoping that by itself told those two to get out and don't even bother knocking on my door. My poor baby was moving around, making it uncomfortable to lay in my bed. No wonder today is the 13th, pure crosses, some real bad crosses at that. Pablo would make anyone's stomach turn even a pregnant one.

"Keisha Lopez you are rude and disgusting! How dear you disrespect Brother DeJan! Not to mention Pablo who use to take care of you. You are very ungrateful. If you think it's easy to raise a child with an imaginary father and then go right ahead." Said my pimp mother hen after barging into my room; guess her guests left and she is now showing her strength.

"Just close my room door behind you, go to your church service and beg God to give you some sense, because it's obvious you don't have none."

"If you weren't pregnant I would give you a good ole Jamaican ass whipping. You were always spoiled rotten that's why your mouth is so fresh and out of order. As soon as you have this baby I need you out, go rent an apartment. Let me see who going to help you, eh perhaps your imaginary baby father's family."

I didn't bother to answer, just waited for her to leave the apartment with her food and stupid backside.

Peace and quiet in the room, in the apartment at that but for some reason my birth canal was on fire. Shoot man, what's going on here? Mother hen left and I am alone. Sharp pain, like contractions. "Dear Jesus, not now!" I yelled, echoing as there wasn't a soul to hear me. Father God who to call? I don't care for Jay being in my business and Roberta is in the Bronx.

Wait, the Superintendent did say if I needed anything to call on him. I am in too much pain to roll down the steps. I did see his number written down somewhere in the kitchen, how do I roll from my room to the kitchen Father God?

Fish out of water, flapping on the floor is the best way to describe my attempt to get to the kitchen. What a torching experience, crawling like a snail when the pain kicks my ass, the flopping away when it subsides for a second or two. All I know for sure my body was in pain and my imagination had me thinking wildly.

"Do you remember telling me if I needed anything I should call you? Well I am here alone in apartment 3J and in labor." I got the Super on the phone after two rings, how lucky for me.

In two shakes he was in my apartment. My head was spinning. I was feeling dizzy. I heard two voices, a familiar voice at that.

***

My head felt heavy and pounding not to mention my back. I don't remember how I got to the hospital, just know I woke up and there are IV's and machine beeping annoyingly. I reached for the call button; it took 5 minutes or so before a nurse's aide came.

"Hi Miss Lopez, my name is Alicia Brooms your nurse's aide. Do you know where you are?"

"From the looks of these tubes I would say the hospital, just not sure where exactly." I answered her riddle or quiz test.

"You were brought in by EMT four hours ago and you are at Kings County Hospital." She informed me. I remember crawling on the floor and calling the Super and then went blank.

"How is the baby? Alicia I am supposed to have my baby at Brookdale not here."

"I will let Charge Nurse Cynthia Pearl know, she will be right in, just give her a few. We have so many new admissions today. Relax in the meantime, I believe there are some people here to see you. I will let them know you are awake."

Visitors? Who could they be, mother is at church unless the Super is still around which I strongly doubt. He wouldn't stick around don't even like drama in the building, a man of few words is what best describes him.

Around 20 minutes after Alicia left a familiar face stuck their head from behind the privacy curtain. Not saying a

word he stood there with a huge smile on his face. I
wanted to pinch myself.

"Hi how are you and the baby doing?"
I wanted to shit this bed up, what on earth was he doing
here?

"We are fine, what are you doing here?" I asked. I don't
even know his name just remembered him from that first
transaction with Phil. He came to the apartment to get the
cakes.

"Good to know, your man sent me to keep an eye on you
and to take you to see him when possible."

"And you are?" I asked him. I wasn't going anywhere with
no hoodlum, this dude better be kidding me.

"Shaggy, that's my name. I am going to leave my number
to text me in code." He said.

"The aide said I had more than one visitor, who else is here
with you Shaggy?"

"Oh the Super, he will stay until your mother comes. I
have to leave though, really don't want people seeing me
around here. Take care and text me if you need anything."

In code, he sounded like a mob leader, or one of their
soldiers. Could it be that Phil had him watching me all
along? My body is already feeling like crap. I don't even
have the capacity to process the entire mob gangster code
situation.

"Good afternoon Miss Lopez, my name is Cynthia Pearl your charge nurse for the next 5 hours of my shift. How are you feeling?"

"Good afternoon nurse. I feel like a set of drums are playing in my head but I am mostly concerned about the baby. How is he doing?"
"Your baby is fine, it's your blood pressure it's a bit high and we will continue to monitor you for the next few days. Try to relax and not worry, the doctors will prefer to induce labor closer to your due date as oppose to now."

"Could you call my mother? She wasn't home when I passed out. I don't want her to panic when she comes home and doesn't see me." I asked, although we argued I know she will worry her size 20 bingo bag panties down to a smaller size, perhaps 8.

This very special Sunday the 13th is a day I will never forget, the day I almost had my firstborn on an unlucky number and the day I had an intrusive intervention. Life, filled with pain, mental pain, pre-labor pain and constant out right pain.

Chapter 14
Your Surname Please

"Tell me what more, what more can Jesus do? What more can Jesus do, Jesus lay the foundation and open up the gates of glory..."

"Ma stop singing!" I yelled from my bedroom. My back was killing me, this little boy decided to come five days after I was admitted and his Grandmother or spoiling second mother is now a recording artiste singing to him, the walls and rodents to sleep. Who knows the disgusting rodents must have been scared from her off key notes. She sure wasn't serenading my soul; more like giving me more discomfort and a possible ear infection. Speaking of which Philippe Lopez is more likely to get an infections as well, something normal for babies anyhow.

"Hush your ass I am singing to my grandson, since you don't love church this little one will be with me every Sunday. Whether at an Orisha feast or bell and water service and another thing very soon brother Dejan will have to offer him up to an Orisha energy."

"Really now Ma, every Sunday? So does this mean I don't have to move out again?" I asked playfully ignoring her mention of offering.

"Philippe is welcome to stay forever, as for you...find your own place in couple months." She answered.

"Whatever." I don't care what she says; my ass will be living here, going to school and getting my life together. Besides seeing one of Phil's soldiers only confirms he is close and not in Jamaica, besides it is usually hard to deport a Don. The streets is saying about 50 Jamaicans and few Trinidadians from around the area were in lock down and facing deportation. So I better stick around to at least hear something from him. I need him, I truly need him for his son's welfare and especially that; I don't even know his last name to put on the birth certificate. What a real shame!

Oh boy what a mess, my life gets worst and more complicated each day. I never use to call upon God in my inner thoughts, however I need him to show me some sign. I may have plans but I need God to execute them with no interruptions. But you know what, this Shango man story mother believes in, might do me some good, spiritual conflict and convenience is one hell of a torcher.

"So ma what are your plans for today?" I asked as she got dressed for church.

"There will be a St. Ann's thanksgiving prayer this afternoon and you know that may run late."

"I will be here alone? Ma you know I need your help with the baby could you stay home today please, your grandson needs you badly." I was kissing her butt real hard, this is my first pregnancy. I helped Roberta with her first born. Now that the shoe is on the other foot, this fit is tight and cutting my circulation off. Cho mon- is how those Jamaicans like to say when they get frustrated. Another life depending on you is no joke indeed.

"Roberta and the kids will be here soon to help give you a hand, all she's asking is that you pay her cab fare."

"I just love how you two always and continue to make plans for my money! Damn you two. I can't wait to move far away from here."

"Don't let me stop you, you ungrateful pickney. I don't see your child's father or his family coming here to give support, so take what you getting and hush your mouth!"

"Go to church, go save your soul and let me worry about being grateful and where my child's father and his family are!" They got on my last nerve. They, meaning Roberta and mother since they don't have a clue about my child's father; every chance they get, they throw it in my face. How sick is that?

Three hours passed and still no sign of Roberta and her clan. So what the hell am I paying for baby sitting or is she up to no good and trying to hustle me? Knowing her, the driver could be her friend who offered to take her here and she's looking for a quick buck to buy a shoes or some dumb shit.

Kiss teeth, and kick rocks. I should be piggy backing from the days I used to care for my newborn nieces and nephews for free. Roberta is a no show, lazy and unreliable dysfunctional character.

Hold up who could that be at the door? She has keys to the front door and the apartment as well? But I am not surprised, thought mom changed the locks and vowed never to give her a spare. Cho talking about my weak mother anyway.

"Open up, it's me." The voice on the other side of the door answered.

"Well 'me' needs a name of some sorts." I pressed for more information. I wasn't about to let any strange punk inside who could harm me and the baby.

"The Super, hurry I got company." His voice softened, I could tell he didn't want the nosy neighbors to hear or to peep through their door hole.

My heart beat with excitement. I haven't seen Phil in almost a year. I knew he could show up but not this soon.

The Super walked into the living room, while Phil held my hands and took me into the kitchen for privacy.

"How have you been? How is the baby?" Phil asked with a great sense of nervousness. I could tell him being in my apartment was a huge risk. Almost like a breach in security, just like when there is a slip up at the Pentagon. He was making me shaky as well. I couldn't find words to answer him immediately. I did however felt the tears running down my cheeks.

"Stop crying, I know you needed me. But I had no idea you were pregnant Keke. Let me be there for you from now on. But first you and the baby have to move from Brooklyn and I will provide a place in Long Island."

"Long Island, why so far?" I asked. He was saying the right things, just not the right place. In some twisted way I needed my mother to help me with Philippe.

"I will explain when we are safe to talk. There is so much I have to share with you Keke, so much." He was calm but yet scared. Being back in the 90's is like coming back to be killed. A fallen King or in the Jamaica slang, a fallen Don should never return to his former palace.

"We cannot leave Brooklyn without you signing his birth paper. At the very least I need him to have your true identity, not just only mine.

"Ok I will take care of it. I have people working at the hospital who will handle the paper work discreetly. Now can I see him?"

"Sure, he is sleeping so look and don't touch." I instructed him.

Leading Phillip into the bedroom to see his son, quietly we tiptoed and looked at him sleeping peaceably. The Super made himself comfortable flipping the channel on the flat screen TV. Phillip was pleased. His son was the splitting image of him, absolutely no DNA test needed here!

From the look on his face I could tell Phil was elated! He held me by the waist and began kissing me gently. There weren't any words between us, just a bonding moment of silence, very intense but yet romantic to some extent. I remember Jay telling me he has another child with some lady couple blocks from me. I am not sure how to feel or think about him anymore. Should I really listen to his advice and move out and be closer to him in Long Island? There is so much to learn about Phil.

"I have to go now." He said as his cell vibrated. Guess there was a look out man watching his back or something. I said nothing just kept still and as he kissed me on the lips, I didn't give in. It felt so painful and I wanted him to know.

"Here is couple thousand to help you move. If you need to get message to me just let the Super know. The sooner you move Keke the more help I can be to you and my son. I truly want what's best for you two."

Something about his words seemed sincere, but he wasn't acting right. Phil was now a softy, not the former Don of the 90's would be with a chip on his shoulder, no he was hiding something or up to something. Whichever I am not comfortable with him just calmly demanding me to move because he says so. I already have my plans to move out, not to no Long Island for sure and start cosmetology school in 6 months. Pablo tried dictating my life and you saw where that got him. Now Phil, although I had feelings for him at bit different from Pablo, I don't know him and then again it's not like you could pull up a chair and sit inside someone's brain to get a front row seat and know them completely. God or the Orishas never made this possible. His disappearing and then reappearing act wasn't cutting it.

One would think seeing Phil would have made me happy but it only made my head ache with thoughts and the feeling as though a drummer was having a party on the right side of my head. These nosy clan, who are unfortunately my family was another reason for my head trauma, cho mon. Literally within seconds after Phil and the Super left the apartment, Roberta showed up. She brought more gifts for the baby. I made sure to check it wasn't any hand-me-downs from one of my nephews, or fake name brand items from around-the-way discount store. Man, them street hustlers slogan is, 'The real thing for quarter price homie."

"Berta come here a second please." Well she was getting paid so she was at my beck and call, right.

"What!" She answered with major attitude; this heifer wants my money and giving me stinky.

"Change him and keep him in mama's room. I need some shut eye." A phrase them yardies loved to use. Roberta the baby helper for the day was doing as told and even cooking food for her and the clan of hyperactive kids. Anyways two Tylenols did the trick and I was out and off to dream land.

Chapter 15
Dreams of Sacrifice

Dressed in a red cotton close fitting two piece skirt and top, I felt a hand, a strange hand holding me. I knew his frame, strong and tall but his face wasn't visible. Fear kicked in as he spoke.

"Will you marry me?"

I looked down at my fingers and a gold ring with an oval shaped design was on my left finger. Then suddenly I heard a goat making the sound they do when they are about to be slaughtered. The goat was to the back of me. I turned and looked over my shoulders. All I saw was his head covered in blood and two red candles lit on both sides.

"Wake up Keke, wake up!" mother yelled shaking me. Apparently I was dreaming and screaming out loud in my bed.

"What happened?" she asked.

Horrified by the looks of that bloody goat I slowly recounted the dream. All mother did was bow her head in silence as though she knew the interpretation like Joseph the dreamer from the Bible.

"Relax my daughter, I will explain. I am going to feed your stomach first with some food from yesterday because what I am about to tell you…" she paused gathering her words carefully. "Will either make you a believer or run from me for good."

Lord Jesus not again, not another obeah woman story, about spirit, animal sacrifice and oil down or perfumes to help ward off spirits or even sometimes mother would say these items are used to entertain them. Right now all I care about is my son and my life getting somewhere.

After I stuffed my face I made up some lame story and told mother I wasn't up to listening to another interpretation. She was ok with what I told her, besides she was too busy with Philippe to even force my ears to listen.

I had gotten use to these dreams, ever so often I had one of these visions, well strange sleeping experiences after telling her about them. She would either burn incense or a candle or spoke some weird language before doing some ritual. Mother's spiritual beliefs was her prerogative not mine and I love her for being so focused and extremely committed to her belief system.

Goat killing, chicken killing only God knows what other animal mother and her clan sacrificed over the years. Personally I don't care. I don't judge what I don't know or care to understand especially when it doesn't affect me directly. The only thing I didn't like was couple weeks before I gave birth to Philippe; mother asked me to accompany her to see Brother DeJan. Needless to say they had an offering of 4 fouls. I took a backseat and watch the entire prance and shout. Women's bodies being transformed, or possessed is more like it. Doing and saying weird things and yes being the odd one made each manifestation attend to me. They did mark my forehead with animal blood. Brother DeJan said it was ok, not to worry. Yeah right his very repetitious words.
"We have to go to Trinidad!" Mother barged into my room demanding I take her seriously.

"Ma respect my privacy please, suppose I was in here playing with a dildo?"

"Chile hush your mouth and listen. I haven't been able to sleep since you had that dream five days now."

"So what does that have to do with me going to Trinidad?"

"You don't want to make the goat offering here and the only option is Trinidad where Brother DeJan is from! That's final!"

"No I am not taking my newborn to some strange tropical island to catch infections and to be bitten by some mosquitoes, besides you from Jamaica why not there?"

"Keke trust me on this one."

"Why mother? Why should I go to Trinidad? What is so pressing that I must engage in such obeah acts?"

Do you remember when Pablo slapped me across my face like a cricket bat against an 80mph ball? Well mother slapped the sparkling stars to the forefront of my eyes.

"Don't you ever dear let me hear you say that word to my face again! Obeah is what got your ass out of jail, that same obeah kept you from getting into deep shit while running the streets with Pablo. Wait you think I never know what you've been doing?

My face and feelings were stung with embarrassment; mother was great at pretending, a damn good snake if you ask me.

"Whoever Philippe's father is, that man is not good for you! Keke that is what that dreams mean; not sure what your plans are with him since I don't know what he looks like or ever smell like. I strongly recommend you stay far from him, bury all memories of him from your thoughts and feelings of sex!"

Tears running down my cheeks, flooding my pillow as Philippe cried thanks to our arguing. The only thing I could think of is packing my belongings, taking Philippe and heading to Long Island. What has my life become? Why my life is so confusing and emotionally off balance?

Chapter 16
The Mexican Border

"Why the hell you driving so fucking fast man!" Rodriquez was screaming to Raymond. "What do you want? The State Trooper to stop us and take us back to prison?"

"No fool, he won't stop us for sure. I got this. Remember all this was my plan to escape prison, not yours!" My brothers were in Texas, five exits from the border, yes you guessed it, making a run to Mexico. The trooper stopped them and asked for paper work, you know the usual. Raymond the one with the brain, reached inside the glove compartment and took out an envelope with cash. Surprisingly the trooper handed Raymond an envelope as well.

"Your paperwork seems to be in perfect order. Inspector Juan Santos will take you over the border, now slowdown and best of luck to you." Trooper Austin, well that's the name on his badge, who knows if this was his real name. Apparently Raymond paid his way out, some tight in prison connection that was legit on the surface. Since Rodriguez was a nervous wreck, Raymond withheld details from him. As I said earlier Raymond was the calm, cool and collective one of the two.

Chapter 17
Bonding with James Bond

Philippe Gordon, my little man is now 8 months and a handful of excitement each day. After mom slapped the daylight out of me, I decided enough was enough. I asked the Super to help me find an apartment and within days I was out and on my own.

My apartment was a huge two bedroom, decorated with expensive furniture from Macy's; the building was quiet and well kept. I moved to Coney Island, Phil paid the rent each month $950 and gave me $500 for house money. He knew I had savings but didn't stress me, whenever I needed something he gave it to me. Philippe and I saw more of him, now that we lived far away from the 90's. The chances of the men from the hood seeing him was slim, he even slept over a few nights and to my surprise spent a week. Of course I thought it was strange for a dealer like himself to be away from his business shacked up under me for so long. But I welcomed it. I truly got the time to bond and spread my heart gate wide open to his. It was so funny, Phil reminded me of James Bond, just plain out right mysterious and at the end, beds his female co-star after she played hard to get the entire movie.

One thing Phil did point out to me during our bonding conversations, that if I had stayed longer at mother's, then someone would recognize the baby and put us together and that would have sparked some drama, especially the fact he has two baby mother living blocks away from mother's. So my ass would have caught heat from the goonz in the streets, plus his ghetto fabulous war some

Jamaican baby mothers. Trust I witnessed plenty fights with them and other women over their men. "Gyal ah my man so go sit dung, him nuh want you idiot!" Oh my Jesus, some things they said during arguments, were embarrassing to say the very least.

"Baby Philippe has a rash on his left butt cheek Keke that cream you rubbing not working at all." Mother Jennifer said before she left for the day.

Mother Jennifer was from my mother's spiritual circle. She wasn't working and needed to hustle a few bucks to help out with her monthly expenses. So I had her come stay with Philippe while I took classes and worked part-time.

"Thanks Mother Jennifer, I will take him to the Doctor tomorrow morning. She opens on Saturdays and takes walk-ins." I had the weekend off and was grateful for the help. Although I was happy and on my own, I had little experience with raising kids much less a 8 month old baby. So much to learn and I was determined to be the best mother. One thing I loved about Mother Jennifer she never forced her spiritual belief on me; it was apparent she knew everything that was going on between mother and me but she stayed out of it. I could tell that Philippe loved her as well. His face lit up whenever she walked in the room; he damn near stretched his arms out for her to lift him up. He would kiss her and gave her big smiles. Poor mother she was missing out on some good baby loving.

Our Doctor's visit was brief and I got new medication for Philippe. I had to bring him back next week for a follow up. I swear Doctor Hazel Thompson wanted to steal my child; she was this pretty Jamaican immigrant half breed Chinese 5'5 tall lady. My son was becoming a young lady's man, charming his way through life.

Just as I walked up to the last step to my second floor apartment, my cell rang.

"Where were you?" My baby-daddy asked.

"What is your problem?" I answered him.

"You had me worried. I called several times and your phone kept going directly to voicemail."

"Oh, remember I told you that I was taking Philippe to the Doctor? He has a rash on his butt and the cream I bought at the Pharmacy wasn't working."

"Okay, it must have slipped me. So where are you now?"

"I am about to step inside the apartment, why?"

"Get dressed and pack your bags for the weekend. A driver will pick you and the baby up in an hour."

"For what reason may I ask, Phillip Gordon?" I rarely called him by his Government.

"There you go again, calling out my Government what's wrong with you? You women just love to have your own way! Girl it's Memorial Day weekend and I wanted you and the baby to spend it out here in Long Island with me."

"Only the three of us in your all white house Phil?"

"Yes FBI Agent Keisha Lopez! Sometimes you ask too many questions."

"Phil whatever. See you in a few bye I am hanging up."

"Cool, oh boy do I have a surprise for you."

"I can't wait babes…I have to go and pack as per your orders, so bye now."

Philippe was getting sleeping and annoyed, can't blame him we got up and out the house real early. I put him in his crib while I packed for our weekend getaway with his father. The phone rings, oh bloody Jane no peace for my poor ears, hope that's not Phil bugging the hell out of me. Looking at my watch I had another 20 plus minutes before the driver gets here.

"Hello Mother Jennifer. How you doing?" I answered the phone before it went to voicemail.

"I am ok, how is the baby? What did the Doctor say?" She asked with such concern.

"Little Phil is fine, sleeping right now. Actually we just got home from the Doctors and I am trying to get settled for the holiday weekend. How are you doing?" I asked to be polite.

"I am good, just waiting on the driver to take us to the airport." She answered.

"Oh yeah you never mentioned you were traveling, where are you off to Mother Jennifer?"

"Well Keisha you weren't supposed to know. Your mother and few of the members along with Brother DeJan are heading for Trinidad. Your mother has a goat business to take care of and I have said enough about the matter now. So do take care and I will see you on Wednesday."

"Wednesday; why not Tuesday?"

"My flight coming in late on Monday and that was the other thing I was to tell you. My blood sister Minerva, we share same father but we call her Sister Mini Blake will take care of the baby for me on Tuesday."

"Ok, well have her call me before Monday so we can talk about a few things, since I never met her."

Although Mother Jennifer was thoughtful I wish she did at least let me know in advance. Anyways no need crying over spilled milk, Phil's driver will be here in any minute.

As for mother and her spiritual antics guess she didn't need me in Trinidad after all; all that fuss and yet I am not boarding a plane with her right now.

***

On the way to Long Island, I changed Philippe twice as the Doctor recommended I kept him as dry as possible. Little man was all smiles when he saw his dada. Yes his first words the other day, dada. Phil was all smiles and his ego chest grew big and looking and touching me in places as if he wanted to make another. Guess hearing dada made him go coco for cotton candy.

"Took you long enough Keke, I could have ran a marathon or two." Phil said with a tone as if he wanted the driver to fly over the cars like an airplane.

"It's not too late and for your information Phil, it's the weekend and a holiday weekend at that, traffic backed up for miles without end on the Belt-Parkway. Plus I didn't have enough pampers for the baby so I had the driver stop at the Drug Store."

He walked me and Philippe in from the driveway and helped with my overnight pull on mini-suitcase.

"What did you pack? This thing is heavy Miss Top Model." He asked as if he wasn't use to carrying heavy things. I didn't even bother to answer; besides we argued like two old married couple from the 60's era.

As I walked into the living room area I was greeted with smiling faces. Would you believe strange faces at that? About 15 people were sitting around drinking and having a good time, while the grill gave off jerk smokes. Phil actually has people in this all white house? I am completely shocked!

"Hi Keisha, this little handsome baby must be my nephew Philippe? Come to Aunty Veronica." She gently took my child from my arms. It's a good thing he wasn't a miserable easily crying baby because he would have put up a fight.

"Sorry about that Keisha, my family wanted to meet you so I decided to surprise you with a Bar-Be-Que." Phil now realized the numbness and not to mention the awkward look on my face. I was lost, so many times I have been here in this great big white house with a man who never talked about his relatives not to mention his countless children from the 90's. For all I know these people could be hired actors. I never saw a photograph of any family member not even of his mother.

"Keisha we heard so much about you and the baby, finally we get to meet you." Another person said from the kitchen.

"Same goes here and you are?" What the hell, she already knew my name why not ask for hers.

"I am Carol, Phil's oldest sister. Our mother Precious is taking a nap upstairs in the Guest bedroom. Come on give me a hug; we don't bite." These people sure had a heavy Jamaican tongue. They chopped up the accent real hard and fast. I had to slowly process their words. Good thing I was a mixed breed or else I would be in a maze; not even the Marines could find me in the deepest part of the ocean.

We had lengthy grilling conversations. His sisters were friendly and wanted to kidnap my son. Well not over my dead body. Philippe was a charmer, he kissed and played with their tits. It sure was nice meeting them, a very good surprise. His mother was the best. She talked to me as though we met some years ago. I began to wonder if she was mixing me up with another baby mother, because only God knows why Phil was reenacting the 12 tribes of Israel story. Sprinkling seeds, watering, nourishing and growing them with large monthly allowances.

"We all live in Connecticut and will travel back tonight." Veronica informed me.

"Oh yeah. Why so soon you guys got here today right?"

"No we've been here since Thursday mid-day to be exact." She explained. Oh so that's why I wasn't able to get him on the phone all day, too busy chauffeuring his relatives around. Phillip Gordon had some explaining to do and trust me I will not let him off the hook so easily.

Chapter 18
Operation Discovery and Escape

Meeting Phil's family was a sign that he was letting me in completely. Wow I am still in shock and it has been more than 12 hours since I met them.

"How are you doing my future wife?" He said seductively as he kissed my ear lobe and rubbed my nipples kind of the same way Philippe was doing to his Grandma and Aunts earlier. Only difference he was looking for milk, while Phil was looking to give me some warm human milk from his pants spout, just like a teapot ready to pour into my tiny cup.

"I don't see a ring so you must be talking to a ghost." I was giving him some lip as usual.

"Whatever come here, let me get some sugar." Phil pulled me close to him as I stood looking through the bedroom French glass door that had a beautiful night sky view. We were alone. Philippe was fast asleep from all the antics earlier. Showing off, smiling and dancing to Reggae and Dancehall music he had a ball I tell you.

"What can I do for you Phil 'Secret Agent' Gordon?" I asked playfully.

"You know the usual, play hardball then give it up nice, wet and warm." My cell rang at the end of his sentence. It was mother calling me from Trinidad, I think. She had a special Shabba Ranks ringtone ' Ting-A-Ling'. I pried my body from Phil's grip and ran towards my pocket book.

124

"Ma are you okay? It's almost midnight what's the emergency?"

"Where are you Keke? Wherever you are right this minute you need to leave there now!" She demanded.

"What the hell is wrong with you woman? How dear you call so late with this bullshit." I didn't give her a chance to respond. I hung up and turned my phone off. Now back to regular schedule before I was rudely interrupted.

"I am back babes. You were calling me your future wife for what reason now?" I wrapped my arms around my man as he stood looking at the moon shining through the window. I tiptoed up and reached for a kiss. He was gone. His thoughts of making love to me went the minute I answered the phone.

Phil's facial expression froze as if he wanted me to share my telephone conversation.

"Who were you talking to?" He asked very sternly.

"My mother she was being her usual self, nothing to highlight or report."

"If we are going to be in a serious relationship you need to trust me as much as I need to trust you Keisha."

"Since you brought up the issue about trust, why didn't you tell me your family was coming? Secondly why do they all know about me and I couldn't say the same about them? Now explain that Mr. Trustworthy."

"That's the least of your worries Keisha, the very least." He answered me very weird.

"Well since you have everything figured out do tell me, tell me exactly what I should be concerned with?"

"Listen Keisha I don't feel like arguing. We had a wonderful day let us not spoil it with an unnecessary argument. I am heading to my office. I need to make a few calls, so there's no need for me to stand in an air tight-tensed room."

"Go ahead Phil run and hide behind your shady business deals. You just like to be in total control. I often ask myself what I am doing with you. Why on earth do I continue to entertain a man with so many dark secrets jeopardizing my life and bringing a child into this world for a criminal?"

Phil shot me a look as if he wanted to kill me. I looked back at him deep in his eyes feeling his disgust at my choice of words. I wasn't leaving his stare. Our eyes were locked into each other's; no more words between us as we stood in the moonlit bedroom. Fighting his emotions, he walked out.

After sitting by the window for about 2 hours, I began to feel a sense of panic and fear. I needed Phil's money to help me escape the life of the hood. I wanted his love to let me feel like a real woman. I had his child that bonded us for life.

Walking up behind me I heard him take deep breaths, not sure what to say or do I figured. You see I never belittled him as a man, never challenged him in a discussion like I did just now.

"Keke, we need to talk." He said so apologetic.

"Go ahead I am listening."

"The whole purpose of you and the baby coming here this weekend was to protect you from what is happening back in Brooklyn." He paused.

"Continue."

"There are things I should have told you a long time ago, things that would have made my life easy and danger free. However I feel for you the minute we started doing business the very day you asked me to flip your money. I saw something about you that was different." He paused again.

I got up and started walking away from him, the suspense was annoying.

"Where are you going?" His tone changed from sincerity to that of a school teacher trying to gain control of an unruly student.

"To check on the baby, this conversation is not going anywhere; you are stalling or coming up with some lies. I am done being with men like you Phil, I am done."

"You don't know what the hell you want! One minute you say I live a secret life but yet my money is good enough to take care of you. Spoil your ass rotten. All I have done was treated you with respect and protect you to some extent."

Stopping in my tracts I began hearing my brother, Raymond's voice inside my head.

"Protection comes at a bloody price. When a man protects a woman it usually means a trap is set and escaping will be extremely difficult." That is when it dawned on me that I am here alone, none of my family members knows my whereabouts and Phil is saying he is protecting me. Oh my God I pray this isn't a trap to kidnap me and my baby!

I began to feel a rush of pressure to my head, holding my forehead I fell to the fluffed carpeted floor; the lights were most certainly out in the room and also in my head.

***

Slowly opening my eyes I could hear my heart beat. I could see my chest inhale and exhale the fresh Long Island air. Turning to my left stretching my arms to hold Phil, he was gone. There wasn't any sign of him sleeping next to me. I crawled out of bed feeling gravity weighing a migraine on my head, yeah like a huge rock. Why is it so quiet? No sound of Philippe's early morning crying for his mother's milk.

Speaking of milk, there was a white coffee mug with steaming black Jamaican Blue Mountain brand coffee which hit my nostrils. I took a sip and it needed more milk and sugar, so I decided to go down and fix this poorly made morning eye opener. Phil was great at being a provider but in the coffee or kitchen department, he sucked for a Jamaican. He truly disappoints.

Wait a second, where is Philippe? It's not like him to be so quiet. Let me go check on him and forget about this coffee nonsense. I got up, wrapped my white silk robe Phil bought me recently along with a pair of white puffy and comfortable Channel bedroom slippers.

I was decked out like a real 'Mob Wife'; 24 karat white gold diamond studs earrings, bracelets and a ring! Wait a minute, where did this ring come from? Did Phil slip this one on while I slept? OMG! It's huge but who gives a girl an engagement ring when she is fast asleep? Mr. Gordon has some explaining to do; well after I give him some morning sweets, this rock deserves at least 4 hours of riding. Oh boy was I happy like a young teenaged girl with an inexpensive popcorn ring.

On my way to Philippe's room, I heard voices coming from Phil's office. I found it very strange as his relatives left last night and we rarely have guests over. Curiosity flushed me immediately. Let me see who these voices belong to. Running my hands down my hips, feeling for my cell phone, hmmm I came up empty. It must be in my pocket book.

"We need the girl Agent Phil. We need to execute Operation Banana Boat before the twins go deep in heading." One male voice said.

"Don't worry about the baby, he will be protected in the system. We just need to take her now. Trust me this bait will work and we will make sure she doesn't get hurt." A female voice spoke. She sounded like she had a great deal of personal history with Phil, while the male voice was more authoritative.

"Look who we have here." A sinister male voice said over my shoulders as he touched me, causing the coffee mug to fall and spill onto Phil's immaculately white wall to wall carpet.

"Take your hands off me; do I know you?" I asked resisting his hands touching me.

"You are very important and famous Miss Lopez." He said very sarcastically.

Looking at him carefully I recognized him. He then ushered me into the room where the others were discussing business. Phil was sitting at his desk and the other two were standing around looking tense. Fearing for my life and freedom, I now recognized these officers. They were the same Federal Agents who arrested me at my cousin's house. What type of shaky, smoky business Phil was up to?

"I see you got yourself a beautiful Spanish one this time around Phil." The female agent said with a smirk on her face.

"And a baby as a package deal. Boy how are you going to explain this one Phil?"
Guess I am a clown Phil and these agents know something that I was in complete darkness about. Wait is Phil a snitch? Who the hell is he and why are these officers here talking to him like they are all buddies?

"We should just take her in right now, no need to waste time."

"She's not going anywhere, besides what valid reason do you have to take her anyways?" Phil asked. "Give me a minute with her alone please." They left us alone as he asked.

"Where's my baby Phil? What have you done with him? I was yelling on top of my voice.

"Relax he is safe. There's no need to worry or work up any tension." He answered assuring me, or at least trying to.

"Who are you Phil? What is this some sick joke? Why are Federal Agents here and talking to you as though you are one of them? You are a drug dealer from Brooklyn, are you not?" I felt salty tears running down my cheeks, what type of movie role was I playing? Maybe it is *the naïve pretty Spanish girl.*

"Keisha I was trying to explain last night but you kept on arguing about foolishness and then you past out." He paused waiting for me to say something. I was numb; my stomach was in a knot. I felt weird as though someone else was in my body, my head and somewhere along the line my senses had escaped me. I stood, shaking with fear.

"I work for the Feds…your brothers escaped prison and we are going to use you as bait for them to surrender." Phil chose his words carefully. I was sucked into a web, a web that wasn't just illegal activities and filthy money but one that was organized by the Feds! What kind of shit is this?

"Feds, did I hear you correctly?" My knees buckled causing me to hit the floor. I was out and this time. I hope it was for good.

25777438R00075

Made in the USA
Middletown, DE
09 November 2015